At the sight of Molly chattering baby talk to his daughter, something turned over in Ethan's chest.

Some nameless emotion that felt so right and good that he wanted to laugh out loud. She hadn't held Laney long, but the fact that she'd held her at all was important, both to her and to him. She needed to know that he trusted her with his child. And he needed to know she cared.

The admission hit him square in the chest.

"I'm glad you came over."

"Me, too." The TV flickered. He had no idea what programs had come and gone in the past two hours. And he didn't care. Talking to Molly, listening to her laugh, sharing his day with her, was far more pleasurable than any television show.

He wasn't lonely. Didn't have time to be, but whenever Molly wasn't around, something seemed to be missing....

Books by Linda Goodnight

Love Inspired

In the Spirit of...Christmas #326
A Very Special Delivery #349

LINDA GOODNIGHT

A romantic at heart, Linda Goodnight believes in the traditional values of family and home. Writing books enables her to share her certainty that, with faith and perseverance, love can last forever and happy endings really are possible.

A native of Oklahoma, Linda lives in the country with her husband, Gene, and Mugsy, an adorably obnoxious rat terrier. She and Gene have a blended family of six grown children. An elementary school teacher, she is also a licensed nurse. When time permits, Linda loves to read, watch football and rodeo, and indulge in chocolate. She also enjoys taking long, calorie-burning walks in the nearby woods. Readers can write to her at linda@lindagoodnight.com, or c/o Steeple Hill Books, 233 Broadway, Suite 1001, New York, NY 10279.

A Very Special Delivery

Linda Goodnight

Published by Steeple Hill Books™

STEEPLE HILL BOOKS

ISBN 0-373-81263-9

A VERY SPECIAL DELIVERY

This edition published by arrangement with Steeple Hill Books.

www.SteepleHill.com

Printed in U.S.A.

There is now therefore no condemnation
to them that are in Christ Jesus.

—*Romans* 8:1

In memory of
(Bubby) Joseph Kayne Matthews

Chapter One

A wintry mix of freezing rain, sleet and snow peppered the roof and rattled the windows of the old farmhouse. Icy tentacles of cold snaked beneath the door to rush across the hardwood floors and over the gray cat sleeping on the colorful oval rug. Molly McCreight shivered, laid aside her book, and rose from her cozy spot in front of the blazing fireplace. The cat stirred, too, gazing up with curious green eyes.

"Ah, be still, Samson. I'm just going to poke something against that door. If Bart Crimshaw had fixed it last summer like he was supposed to..." She let the words and thoughts drift away. Bart, the beast, hadn't ever done anything he was supposed to do.

He'd disappeared like all the others as soon as he realized she wasn't kidding when she said she would never be interested in having children.

"But we don't care, do we, Samson? We're doing fine, just fine, without any of them."

The cat's ears flicked, though he stayed beside the glowing fire. She wasn't doing just fine and even Samson knew it. She mourned for the loss of her once-close relationships with her mother and her sister, Chloe, and most of all, she mourned for baby Zack.

Since she'd taken the job at the Winding Stair Senior Citizen Center things had been a little better, but the estrangement from her family still lay like a rock in the pit of her stomach.

As she mumbled to the bored-looking cat, Molly took a towel from the bathroom, rolled the thick terrycloth like a jelly roll and stuffed it under the front door.

"Listen to that wind." Hunching her shoulders, she rubbed her upper arms as if to ward off the outside chill. "It's a miracle we still have electricity."

Above the incessant howl of winter came a low hum.

"What in the world?" Molly pulled the heavy antique-rose drape away from the window and peered out. Though the time was not yet six o'clock, outside was as dark as sin. "Surely, that's not a vehicle way out here in this storm?"

Thick layers of ice already coated the windows, the porch and the front of the house. More of the icy pellets and rain fell in such abundance she was hard-pressed to make out the faint glow of lights in the distance. The hum of a motor increased, coming closer. Since her farmhouse sat a ways off the main gravel road, Molly knew the visitor was headed in her direction.

When the freezing rain had begun early that morning, she had done the sensible thing and prepared for the certain storm ahead. She'd filled the wood box and piled enough extra wood on the porch to keep her going for days even though the propane tank was full. She'd run water into buckets though the water had never frozen in the two years she'd lived on the remote farm in Oklahoma's Kiamichi Mountains. And she'd made a pot of vegetable beef stew to die for just because the rich aroma of stewed tomatoes and beef filtering through the house made her feel warmer.

"Looks like a truck of some sort," she muttered, frowning through the narrow window in the front door. She flipped on the porch light and strained her eyes against the darkness camped beyond the yard.

"It *is* a truck, Samson. A delivery truck." Her frown deepened. "Now, what kind of idiot…?"

The headlights disappeared as if they'd been sucked inside the dying motor. A smaller light signaled the opening of the van door. With a muffled thud, that light was extinguished also.

Molly made out the hurrying form of a man, not overly tall, but not short either, picking his way over the crusty ice toward her front porch. Bundled against the frigid weather, he looked thick and heavy but moved with speed and agility, his arms crossed in front of him in a posture Molly found odd for running.

He was carrying something. At times, she ordered a lot of things, but come on.

"No package could be that important."

When the man's feet thudded against the wooden porch, Molly yanked the door open, gasping at the sudden blast of frigid air.

Shadowed beneath the glowing yellow light with sleet and bits of snow swirling around him, the man peered down at her from under a brown bill cap. He was a uniformed delivery man, all right. She recognized the familiar dark brown truck that sailed up and down the country roads delivering packages. The man himself looked vaguely familiar, but he wasn't her usual delivery man.

"Ma'am, I was wondering if you could—"

She didn't give him a chance to finish. The cold air was filling up her cozy little house, and she wasn't about to stand on ceremony in this kind of weather. He couldn't be a criminal. Even an ax murderer had better sense than to be out in this weather. Only a working stiff would be so dedicated.

"Get in here before you freeze." With one hand she shoved the storm door wide and with the other she grasped his thick, quilted sleeve and pulled. That's when she realized what he was carrying against his chest. Not a package. A bundle. A soft, quilted bundle decorated with yellow ducks and pink rabbits. She yanked her hand away and stared long and hard as the delivery man stomped into the house, sprinkling ice pellets all over the floor. He ushered in the unmistakable scent of cold air on a warm body.

Molly shut the door and kicked the towel against it, all the while staring in disbelief at the bundle in the delivery man's arms.

The man went straight for the fireplace and stood close, his back to her. Molly followed him, keeping her eyes on the bundle. Maybe it wasn't what she thought it was.

"The roads are so bad, I was afraid I wouldn't make it back to town. Don't need to tell you what would happen if I got stranded and ran out of gas in this weather."

"No."

There would be enough horror stories in the days to come of motorists or other hapless folks who'd gotten caught out in this. The occasional Oklahoma ice storms were notorious for paralyzing entire sections of the state. Sometimes weeks would pass before the roads were cleared, power back on, and life returned to normal. Aunt Patsy, the farm's true owner, had spent her share of days stranded up here while waiting for the ice to melt or the road grader to arrive in this remote portion of the county.

"I'm sorry to intrude on you this way." A pair of sincere blue eyes—worried eyes—

peered at her. Normally she would have considered such eyes, rimmed as they were in black spiky lashes, especially attractive. And the rest of his face—clean-shaven, lean and honest—was only made more ruggedly attractive by a narrow scar that sliced one eyebrow and disappeared upward into a neat crew cut. She found the scar intriguing—and appealing.

The bundle in his arms was an entirely different matter.

"You're the closest house for miles," he said, as though that gave him the right to remind her of what she could never forget.

Most times she loved the solitude of living miles from nowhere, driving in to her job and then hurrying home to her little farm. In town she could always feel the stares, the eyes of suspicion, and hear the not-so-subtle whispers. No matter that the tragedy happened two years ago, a small town never forgot—or forgave—such a terrible transgression. How could they when she couldn't even forgive herself?

"You got a telephone?"

Her gaze flickered up to his and quickly back to the bundle. Yellow ducks and pink rabbits. Foreboding crept up her spine, colder than the outside temperatures. "Phone's been out since noon."

"Figures. My communication system is down, too, and cell phones are impossible up here in the hills."

Molly knew that. No one in these mountains even considered buying a cell phone.

Tormented by thoughts of the bundle, she turned her back to the fire and tried not to think too much. *Please, Lord, please. Let that be a doll. Or a puppy.*

The bundle stirred; a soft cooing issued from the quilt. Molly's pulse rate jumped a notch. That was no puppy.

"Ma'am…" the delivery man began.

"Molly," she interrupted, stepping back, terrified of what he was about to say. "I'm Molly McCreight."

"Pleased to meet you, ma'am, and I'm Ethan Hunter." He thrust the bundle toward her. "Do you know anything about babies?"

Her heart stopped beating for a full three seconds. She couldn't breath. There really was a baby inside that mass of quilts and blankets.

In all his thirty-three years, Ethan had never seen a female react this way to a baby.

The red-haired woman turned deathly pale, her brown eyes widened in panic as she backed slowly toward the crackling fireplace behind her. Usually, little Laney was a regular chick magnet, drawing unwanted female attention even when he stopped at the supermarket for a carton of milk or a bag of diapers. But tonight when he actually desired that little bit of magic, the woman in question looked as if she'd rather jump into the fireplace than touch his baby daughter.

"I know this is unusual, ma'am."

"Molly," the woman whispered through white lips, her gaze never leaving Laney's blankets.

"Molly," he tried again. "I'm sorry to intrude on you this way, but I have a delivery that must be made tonight."

Her eyes widened in panic. "Here?"

"No, ma'am. To Mr. Chester Stubbs."

She looked up, interested, concerned, though her blanched face never regained its former peaches-and-cream color. "I know Chester. He lives about as far back into the mountains as you can get and still be on this planet."

"Exactly. And the roads up in there are

little more than winding trails." Every inch of the way from town, over slick and ice-packed roads, he'd prayed, believing with all his might that he was meant to deliver this gamma. For the last half hour he'd prayed to find some safe place to leave Laney. When he'd seen the glow of this farmhouse, the only place for miles, he'd been certain this was the Lord's answer. But now, given Molly McCreight's reluctance, he wasn't so sure.

"Can't the delivery wait until this ice storm thaws?"

"No, ma'am. It's gamma, and gamma can't wait."

Her startled eyes flicked from Laney to him. "What in the world is gamma?"

"A high-powered cancer treatment. Once a patient begins treatment, his infusion must be delivered on time. Gamma's shelf life is only eight hours. More than two hours has already passed since I picked up the gamma from the lab. In six hours Mr. Stubbs will die unless I can get up that mountain."

His declaration sounded overly dramatic to Molly, but she knew Chester was battling cancer. Chester and Mamie Stubbs were one of the nicest couples around, and if Chester needed that treatment, she wanted him to have it. The older couple had been kind to her, showing her what real Christian love and compassion was all about when her own family had turned its back.

"Then you have no choice. Go."

Ethan's shoulders relaxed as he began to unwrap the bundle in his arms.

Fear and a sudden premonition shot up Molly's spine. "What are you doing?"

"Your house is warm. Laney won't need all this cover in here. I'll just lay her in that big chair over there and she'll sleep most of the time I'm gone."

Panic raised the level of her voice. "You're not leaving her here?"

Baffled blue eyes blinked at her. "I thought we just agreed to that."

Molly rasped her tongue over lips that had suddenly gone as dry as baby powder. "I never agreed to any such thing."

"But I can't take her with me. What if I don't make it? What if the truck runs into a ditch?"

Knees trembling, Molly retreated to the other side of the room, placing a fat old easy chair between herself and the baby. She gripped the back, digging her fingers into the thick upholstery—holding on for dear life.

"Why did you bring her out in this weather in the first place?"

"I'm afraid I didn't have a choice in the matter. The daycare closed early because of the storm, and I had no place else to take her."

"Where's your wife?"

The man's face froze as surely as if he'd stayed out on her porch all night. Blue eyes frosted over. He pulled the sleeping bundle a little closer to his chest. "I don't have a wife."

He had a baby but not a wife. Now there was an interesting story she was certain, but not one she cared to explore. Men, especially a man with a motherless baby, were at the bottom of her social calendar.

Molly had only been hysterical once in her entire life—the last time she'd held a baby—and she didn't care to repeat the experience.

"I'm sorry, Mr...Ethan, babies and I don't get along very well. Someone else will have to deliver that medicine to Mr. Stubbs."

Impatience flickered across his face. The rugged-looking scar blanched. "There is no one else."

Molly knew he was telling the truth and

that she was being unreasonable. He'd traveled this far in that truck, but the chances of him getting up that mountain were slim. The chances of anyone else making it this far were practically zero.

"Wait a minute." A sudden thought struck her. "If this gamma stuff is some sort of chemotherapy, who's going to do the infusion? Don't you need a nurse or a doctor for that?"

"Normally, but the home health nurse can't get there."

"What good will the medication be without someone to administer it?"

"I can do the infusion. That's why the company sent me. Otherwise, Laney and I would be safely home for the night."

Molly squinted in consideration. A baby but no wife. A delivery man with medical expertise who was willing to risk his life to make a nearly impossible delivery. Ethan Hunter was as full of secrets as she was.

"Are you a doctor masquerading as a UPS driver?"

She wished she hadn't asked. The handsome lips narrowed to a thin line. The sculpted jaw clenched, blanching the beguiling scar snow-white.

"Look, Molly, a man's life depends on me, and the clock is ticking here. All I'm asking you to do is babysit for a couple of hours. You obviously aren't going out anywhere, and I'll pay you well. Why should that be such a big deal?"

If only he knew, he wouldn't let her within breathing distance of his daughter. But that was a secret she couldn't share with a stranger.

Suddenly too hot despite the frigid temperatures, Molly moved from the fireplace to the window. The ice pellets pecked incessantly at the glass pane like angry birds. In the glow of the yard light, ice glistened on everything in sight. Trees bent low and power lines bowed with the heavy encrustation of ice. In only a matter of time the lines would snap and the power would go.

What could she do? What choice did she have? Chester's life depended on this gamma stuff, and as much as she wanted to argue the point, taking a baby out in this weather was unconscionable. Regardless of her family's accusations, she'd never intentionally cause harm to anyone, especially a child.

She sighed, wishing she'd stayed in town

with Aunt Patsy last night when the first warnings had come about the ice storm.

No, that was selfish. She didn't wish that. She wished she wasn't such a coward.

Ethan Hunter certainly wasn't. This man with the baby was willing to put his own life at risk to help an old man he didn't even know. And he was willing to put his child's life in her less-than-capable hands to do it.

Lord, what a mess. Please help me know what to do.

She dropped into the overstuffed chair and rubbed at shoulder muscles gone as tight as cheap shoes.

"Ethan, you don't even know me. How can you be sure I'll take proper care of your daughter?"

He studied her for a long, serious moment then smiled. Molly's breath caught in her throat. Goodness, gracious and mercy! Ethan Hunter was devastatingly handsome when he smiled.

"The eyes are the windows to the soul. That's what my mama taught me."

"Oh, so my eyes tell you that I'm good with children?"

He came toward her, hunkering down in front of the chair, the baby still in his arms.

"They tell me you're a good person. A little sad, maybe, and real scared of something, but a gentle, caring woman who'll look after Laney with everything in you."

Disturbed by his all-too-accurate assessment, Molly lowered her gaze to the baby, her stomach churning in trepidation. Chester's life hung on her decision. Spending even an hour alone with a baby would be pure torture, but she had no choice. She had to do this. She only hoped the baby's life wasn't in jeopardy, too.

Chapter Two

Molly stood at the window watching as the delivery truck struggled down the driveway, this time leaving her alone with a diaper bag and a small baby. The hazy fog of ice crystals blocked the van from view in no time and the howling wind covered the hum of the disappearing motor. He was gone. And she was alone for the first time in two years with someone else's baby.

She hadn't had a panic attack in the last six months, had believed she was finally past the painful valley of mourning, but she was near the point of panic now. The terror that closed off the windpipe and rattled the pulse wasn't far from taking over. Drawing in a deep breath, she rested her cheek against the frozen windowpane and quoted the scripture Aunt Patsy had made her personalize and memorize. *God has not given me the spirit of fear.*

Even though she still struggled to believe that God was with her, helping her, the scripture somehow calmed her terror. It hadn't at first, but over the months of constant repetition and Aunt Patsy's gentle counsel, she'd slowly gained control over the attacks.

A soft mewling sound issued from behind her. Whirling, hand at her tight throat, Molly hurried to the couch. True to his word, Ethan had moved the chair against the sofa and organized the cushions so that the baby wouldn't fall, but he'd been wrong about her staying asleep. Wide awake, blue eyes gazing up at Molly, the child gnawed at a tiny pink fist.

"God has not given me the spirit of fear," she mumbled as she pulled a straight-backed chair next to the couch to be near the baby. Maybe if she watched the child every second nothing terrible would happen.

The baby kicked and gooed, squirmed and sucked at her fist, but she didn't go back to sleep. Molly sat rigidly, afraid to move, afraid even to blink. After fifteen minutes her neck muscles ached and she needed to go to the bathroom, a dilemma that meant leaving the baby alone—unthinkable—or picking her up—terrifying. The last baby she'd touched had been dead.

Her scalp prickled from the memory. Baby Zack, his little body still warm, limp and lifeless against her chest as she ran screaming, screaming into the front yard of her sister's house. Neighbors had come running, she didn't know where from, though it was late summer when folks still enjoyed puttering in their gardens and cooking outside. One man carried a garden hoe to frighten away an attacker. But there was no attacker. And all the concerned neighbors in Winding Stair, Oklahoma, couldn't help baby Zack.

The panic started to crawl up Molly's spine once more. Her grip on the chair would surely leave the imprint of her fingers in the wood. She had to hold on. She could not suffer a panic attack while this child was in her care.

No telephone to call for help. No Aunt Patsy to talk her through. This time she'd have to rely on God alone.

A glance at the anniversary clock resting on the fireplace mantel told her that Ethan had been gone all of thirty minutes. At this rate she'd be crazy before he returned.

She refocused her attention on the baby. With a jolt, she saw that Laney's eyes were now closed. Was she asleep or—? The awful thought forced her to do what she dreaded most. Fingers trembling, she reached out, slowly, slowly, and laid a hand on the flannel-clad chest.

A shudder of relief rippled through her at the gentle rise and fall of the sleeping baby's ribcage. Some nameless emotion stirred in Molly's chest at the soft feel of an infant. Even the smell of her, that wonderful baby mixture of milk and lotion, made Molly's chest ache with longing.

Until Zack's death she'd always dreamed of getting married and having a big family. Lots of kids. That's what she'd told everyone. But now that would never happen. Her sister Chloe's healthy, perfect six-month-old son had died while in her care. She must have done something wrong. Or maybe she hadn't watched him closely enough. That's what her sister had said the last time Molly had tried to ask forgiveness.

As much as she'd wanted children, she could never take such a chance again. Chloe was right. Babies just weren't safe with her.

Rubbing gentle circles on the chest of the one now in her care, Molly felt an undeniable sense of loss.

"You sure are a pretty thing," she whispered.

Dark eyelashes curled against rose-over-ivory cheeks, and her round face was topped by a cap of fine, dark hair. Molly couldn't help but wonder about the mother. What had happened to her? And why had Ethan's face gone all tense when Molly had asked about her?

Healthy and well cared for, the baby looked to be about three or four months old, younger than Zack, but not by much. Her pink sleepers, emblazoned with the words Daddy's Girl were clean and neat. Whatever Ethan Hunter's situation with Laney's mother, he loved his little girl.

Samson rose from his spot near the fireplace, stretched his long gray feline body then padded across the room. Before Molly saw what he was about, the cat leaped onto the couch and tiptoed quietly toward the sleeping child.

"Samson, no. Get down."

The cat, as usual, ignored her. He sniffed curiously at Laney's mouth, an act that must have tickled, for the baby's face scrunched up and she turned her head. Suddenly Laney remembered the old wives' tale that a cat could steal a baby's breath.

With more force than she intended, she grabbed Samson and sailed him onto the floor. The shocked animal stared at her in resentment, flicked his tail and stalked to his rug by the crackling fireplace.

Feeling worse than ever, Molly returned to her post beside the sleeping child. Cautiously, she placed her hand on the little chest once again and felt the movements that assured her the baby was breathing. If she had to sit this way all night long, she would. But oh, how she prayed that Ethan Hunter would soon return and take this responsibility off her shoulders.

Nearing midnight, eyes burning from staring into the frozen night, Ethan started back down the mountain. He hadn't reached the Stubbs's remote cabin until nearly nine o'clock, and the grateful couple had fortified him with coffee and brownies while the gamma infused into Chester's blood system.

During those hours with his patient the storm outside had worsened. The world around him was white and crystallized, a fairy tale turned into a nightmare. Chester and Mamie Stubbs had invited him to spend the night, but he'd refused. Laney was waiting. And from Molly's reaction to his child, she was waiting, too—waiting for him to return and take the baby off her hands.

A mighty gust whipped across an open pasture and the van rocked precariously.

Ethan couldn't remember ever driving—or flying—in an ice storm of this caliber. Since leaving the Stubbs's farm he'd stopped over and over again to break ice off his windshield wipers. The delivery van wasn't made to handle these conditions, and even chains on the tires wouldn't have helped on what was now a solid sheet of ice.

Shoulders hunched over the wheel, he stared hard into the night. His headlights reached only a few feet out into the blinding shower of white pellets. He could hardly tell where the road ended and the ditch began. Visibility was next to nothing. During his years as a paramedic helicopter pilot for a medical service he'd grown accustomed to flying by instruments when necessary. Too bad ground transport didn't offer the same technology.

Inch by inch, the van ground slowly forward. Like a shower of tiny rocks, ice tapped relentlessly against the outside. At this rate, he'd be hours getting back to Molly's place. In the past he would have thrown caution to the wind and taken the necessary risks, but no more. Speeding up was a deadly game, and he had a baby waiting for him.

Since the moment Twila had told him she was pregnant, Laney had become his sole focus in life. Though he'd felt safe in doing so, he disliked leaving her with Molly McCreight, a woman who obviously didn't embrace the idea of caring for an infant. His jaw tensed, remembering Laney's mother. What was the matter with women these days? Weren't females naturally supposed to enjoy babies?

He sighed heavily and squinted into the darkness. Maybe not. Maybe his was an old-fashioned dream. Just because his mother was a nurturer whose life had revolved around her kids, didn't mean modern women felt the same. Mom was from a different era when home and family mattered.

He'd had no choice but to leave Laney at the warm, safe farm. Even though she didn't want Laney there, Ethan knew in his heart Molly McCreight would take good care of her. He didn't know how he knew, but he knew. His baby was in good hands.

Ice-coated wipers scraped across the windshield, doing little good, even with the defrosters blasting constant heat. Time to stop again and clear them off. The window, too, was coated in ever-thickening sleet. Easing to a crunching halt, he put the truck in Park, and took the can of de-icer and the ice scraper from the seat beside him. As he leaped from the truck the ice pellets hit him with the force of a sandblaster, driving into his cheeks and neck. He shuddered once, hunched his shoulders against the cold before setting to work.

The world around him was a foreign place. Fence lines had disappeared and electric poles leaned threateningly. Before long there would be few landmarks to guide him. He'd have to be very careful.

"Just me and You, Lord," he said, and the wind slammed ice against his teeth.

In the few short months since he'd become a Christian he'd said those words plenty of times. And now, as every time, he'd felt that calm assurance that he was not alone. No matter what happened, God would be here with him.

Windshield cleared for the moment, he slammed back into the warm truck and dropped the gear into Low. The wheels spun but the van didn't move. Accelerating slightly, Ethan felt the tires start to slide sideways. He fought against the skid, used every bit of his considerable expertise to bring the vehicle under control, but the ice was too much. In seconds, one side of the van tilted sideways into a ditch he hadn't even known was there.

With a sinking sensation in the pit of his stomach, Ethan got out to survey the situation.

The van was hopelessly stuck. The Stubbs' place was at least four miles back. He'd never be able to walk that far in this weather. But he couldn't stay here either. No one would be along this road for days, maybe weeks.

He had little choice but to walk to Molly McCreight's farmhouse, even though he wasn't sure how far that was. With a heavy sigh of dread, he bundled himself as much as possible for the trek, took the flashlight from beneath his seat and stepped out into the wretched storm. He gasped as a sharp north wind slammed into him. Tears stung his eyes.

Less than ten minutes later ice encrusted his eyelashes and obscured his vision. He scraped at them, but his gloves, too, were covered with a fine layer of ice. Several times he slipped and nearly lost his footing, but he trudged on, keeping his focus on getting back to the baby he loved more than life itself. Thinking of Laney had given him the strength to do a lot of difficult things in the past year, and he thanked God every day for the gift of his daughter.

Molly McCreight's pinched face came to mind. He'd liked her the minute she'd pulled him into her house, welcoming him without even asking his business. And he'd liked her house. The neat country hominess—if that was a word—and the tantalizing fragrance of food cooking had reminded him of his parents' home.

He'd thought she was cute, too, with those brown-gold eyes and a sprinkle of freckles across her small nose. But from her reaction to his daughter, Molly was no different than Twila Thompson.

Still, there was something about her that appealed to him. And thinking of Molly and Laney safe and warm in the old farmhouse helped him keep moving.

Bending his neck against the north wind, Ethan shone the flashlight around him. No lights. No houses. Nothing. The flashlight danced wildly. For the first time, he noticed he was shivering and wondered when that had begun. His feet moved more slowly now, too. Even filtered through a muffler, the air hurt his lungs, burning so badly he could hardly stand to draw another breath. The scar over his eye throbbed painfully.

He'd never been this cold before. With every step, sparks, like frozen electricity, shot through his feet. Ethan considered this a good sign. They weren't frostbitten—yet.

He had no idea how far he'd walked, but he did know one thing for certain. Hypothermia was setting in. If he didn't find shelter soon, he'd freeze to death.

The idea sent a surge of adrenaline into his bloodstream. Nothing could happen to him. Baby Laney depended upon him. He was all the parent she had.

"Just me and You, Lord," he muttered through stiff, numb lips.

Snow and ice swirled around him, punishing him with every step, but the warm presence of God strengthened him.

He'd gone less than fifty more feet when he spotted the feeble glow of yellow against the raging white night. Had he not been so cold and miserable, he'd have shouted for joy.

He turned toward the light, trudging, struggling against the bitter wind and within minutes stumbled onto the now-familiar wooden porch.

Without bothering to knock, he shoved open the door. And fell face first into Molly McCreight's arms.

Molly wasn't sure whether to scream in fright or praise God that Ethan Hunter was still breathing. He weighed a ton compared to her, and most of that weight was now shifted to her shoulders. She half dragged, half walked him to a big blue easy chair. Shudders racked his body. His skin was red and windburned. The ice frozen on his eyelashes tore at her heart.

Where was his van? Had he had an accident? Had he made it to Chester's place?

"Ethan." He was by far the most nearly-frozen human being she'd ever seen, but she saw no sign of other injuries. "Are you all right? What happened?"

Stiff lips replied, "Heat exhaustion."

Molly held back a smile. Interesting man to joke under such dire conditions.

"I'll get something hot for you to drink. Stay right here."

Then she laughed at her own silliness. The man could barely move. After a quick glance at the baby, Molly hurried into the kitchen and shoved a cup of instant cocoa into the microwave. While the drink heated, she turned on the flame beneath the pot of beef stew. Ethan would need some hearty, hot food, too. Then she could find out what had happened.

At the beep, beep of the microwave, Molly grabbed the thick brown mug and rushed back to the stranger in her living room. His head lay back and his eyes were closed, but he opened them the minute she reappeared.

She offered him the steaming, rich-scented cocoa.

With a shake of his head, he spoke through chattering teeth. "Too shaky. I'll spill it."

Perplexed, Molly thought for a moment. He absolutely had to get warm—and fast. Ethan would be sick if she didn't get him warmed up soon. If he fell ill in her house so far from town, she'd be left to care for him and his infant daughter. And for her peace of mind, she wanted him and his baby out of here as soon as possible.

What he needed was a good hot bath to chase off the chill, but the idea of offering such a personal thing to a stranger was out of the question. The next best alternative was an electric blanket—and she did have that.

"Will you be okay for a minute?"

"Sure." His ice-encrusted eyelids fell shut. His red-blue lips barely moved.

"I'll get some blankets, but first let's move you closer to the fire."

Grabbing his ice-coated arm, she pulled as he heaved upward. They stumbled to the chair she'd pulled as close as possible to the blaze. As Ethan collapsed once more, he muttered, "Laney?"

What a great dad. Even half-frozen, he still worried about his baby. "She's asleep."

Molly gazed down at him for a second, curious to know more about a man strong enough to risk himself for someone else but tender enough to care for a tiny baby girl.

He was definitely different than most men she knew.

"I'll be right back," she said.

In winter the back of the big, rambling house was closed off to preserve fuel. A trip into the frigid space was always made in haste, so in minutes, she was back in the living room, loaded with blankets.

Ethan remained inert, but his chest rose and fell in exhaustion. The ice attached to his hair and clothes had begun to thaw. Small puddles formed around his feet. Damp spots appeared on his jacket and hat. His leather gloves dripped onto his pant legs.

"You need to get out of that jacket and hat," Molly said, reaching for the stocking cap. It came away, leaving behind a rumpled mess of brown hair.

Ethan roused enough to struggle with his gloves.

"Your fingers are numb. Let me." Without considering the familiarity of such an action, Molly pulled the stiff, wet gloves from his hands, fretting over the reddened, icy fingers as she reached for the zipper on his jacket.

At her touch, Ethan's hand stayed hers. "I got it."

Suddenly embarrassed and more than a little self-conscious, Molly whirled toward the pile of blankets. Behind her, she heard the rustle of his jacket as she plugged in the electric blanket.

"Sorry about the mess."

"Don't be silly." Molly draped the blanket around his shoulders, adding two others for insulation and an old quilt around his legs. "We'll have you warmed up in no time."

"Appreciate it." His head fell back against the old stuffed chair that had been her late uncle Ray's favorite reading spot.

Gradually, Ethan's shudders subsided and he grew still. Except for the crackle of burning logs and the constant onslaught of sleet pecking at the windows, the room was unnervingly quiet.

She wanted to turn on the television, check the weather, but worried the noise might disturb the baby.

A jolt of fear, as powerful as an electrical shock, ripped through her.

The baby.

She had been so preoccupied with the

near-frozen Ethan that she'd momentarily forgotten Laney. Was she all right?

Knees going weak, throat dry as talcum powder, Molly was afraid to look at the makeshift baby bed.

Her breath grew short and her heart rate accelerated as the beginnings of a panic attack threatened.

Ethan was in no shape to take care of himself, much less a baby. How could she be so stupid, so incompetent to forget that a baby was in her care after what had happened to Zack?

"God has not given me the spirit of fear." Approaching the couch, mind flashing photos of a dead child, she clasped a hand against her throat, panting.

A pair of midnight-blue eyes blinked up at her from amidst the yellow-and-blue bunny blankets.

Molly, limp with relief, melted to the floor beside the sofa. Laying her forehead against the cushions, she thanked God that little Laney had suffered no ill effects from her neglect.

She was still there, attention glued to the baby, when Ethan began to stir. He thrust off all but one blanket and stood up.

"Man, do I feel better."

As Molly looked up, her heart leaped wildly. He looked better, too. The UPS driver, scar and all, was a hunk!

"You aren't shaking anymore."

"No, but you are." He frowned down at where she knelt beside the couch. "And you're pale. Are you okay?"

Molly pushed up from her spot on the oval rug and ran sweaty palms down the sides of her sweatpants. "Fine. How about that cup of cocoa now?"

Anything to avoid the subject of why she was so afraid of a tiny baby.

"Sounds good." Weariness emanated from him. If she'd known him better and the situation had not been so serious, Molly would have teased him about the hot-pink blanket draped around his broad shoulders—an incongruous sight if ever there was one.

"How about a bowl of beef stew with that cocoa?"

"Did anyone ever tell you you're a nice lady?"

"I take it you haven't had supper?"

"Coffee and brownies, but they're long gone."

"Did you get all the way up to Chester's?"

He nodded his head. "Yes, thank God."

"It couldn't have been easy."

"No, but my part was a lot easier than Chester's. He's one tough character."

Still, Molly couldn't help but admire Ethan's determination to help another person under such dire circumstances.

The clock had been ticking and Chester's life had depended upon Ethan—and the Lord—to get the medication there on time.

Molly hustled into the kitchen, returning in a matter of minutes with the hot meal.

Ethan settled on the end of the couch next to Laney and told Molly about the trip up the mountain, the hours with Chester, and finally about the truck sliding into a ditch.

"Don't know how I made it in that light-bodied van." He shook his head and corrected himself. "Yes, I do. The Lord." He dug into the steaming bowl of soup. "Hot stew sure hits the spot."

Somehow she'd known Ethan was a Christian, though she'd learned the hard way that not all Christians were as self-sacrificing.

But Ethan was a man who took responsibility seriously and didn't give up easily. She liked that about him.

She liked the way he ate, too, like her dad and uncles, wholeheartedly as though he might never eat again. His appreciation of a simple bowl of stew made her smile.

From what little she'd seen, and from the way he cared for his child, Molly thought she could find a lot of things to like about Ethan Hunter.

He took a bite of cornbread, chewed and swallowed. "I hate to ask this of you, but I don't have a way back to town tonight. You wouldn't happen to have a bunkhouse or a barn I could sleep in, would you? Just for tonight, I mean. If my van was here, I could sleep in that, but…" He lifted one shoulder in a shrug.

"There's a barn, but you would freeze out there."

Practical to the bone, impropriety didn't concern Molly, but it would upset Aunt Patsy. She shifted uncomfortably, fretting. Letting a man freeze to death would be a lot worse than letting him spend the night. "I have an extra room in back. There's no heat, but…"

She let her voice trail off, uncertain how to handle the situation.

"No. It wouldn't be right for me to impose

on you that way. If you'll keep Laney inside, I'll take the barn."

Molly jumped. Her windpipe tightened.

"No. That's not a good idea." Her heart thundered in her chest as she searched for a solution. No way could she spend an entire night alone with Laney.

Ethan studied her curiously. "I'm sorry she's so much trouble."

"It's not that—" How did she explain without admitting the ugly truth—that she was a danger to his child. She couldn't, so instead she searched for a viable solution.

"My uncle Robert keeps his fishing camper here during the winter months. It's self-contained and has a small propane heater. It stays cozy and snug once it's warmed up. I'm sure he wouldn't mind if you used it."

Ethan seemed relieved. He placed his bowl on the coffee table. "That will work great. I don't know how I'll ever thank you for this, Molly."

He was the hero, risking life and limb to help a sick man. She was a coward who wouldn't have done anything at all had he not forced her. She suddenly felt ashamed.

He drew in a breath and leaned forward,

forearms on his thighs, palms pressed together. "So if you have that camper key, I'll go check it out, light the stove and such. Will you watch Laney while I go?"

No! As soon as the thought came, shame followed. If Ethan had nearly frozen to death to help someone else, surely she could find the courage to stay in a warm house with his baby for a few more minutes. She swallowed back the knot of anxiety. She could. She had to.

Pushing out of her chair, Molly went to the bedroom. When she returned with the camper keys clenched in one hand, Ethan was changing Laney's diaper.

She stopped dead in her tracks and watched. Something about a big, masculine man maneuvering a diaper around the chubby, thrashing legs created an endearing scene.

Ethan looked up and grinned, and Molly's heart fluttered oddly.

"She leaks like a sprinkler system." Deftly, he smoothed the plastic tabs into place before slipping the tiny legs into the pajamas.

"You're good at that."

"Practice." He lifted the infant in his big

hands and laid her against a wide, blanket-covered shoulder, patting the tiny back with a tenderness that stirred Molly. One of his hands covered Laney's entire back.

"She's beautiful." Molly swallowed a lump and wished for what could never be.

"Yeah."

To break the spell of man and baby, Molly stuck out her hand, displaying the keys. "The camper is behind the detached garage. The propane bottle is still hooked up so all you have to do is light the stove. You can take these blankets with you."

"Perfect." He took the keys and rose, bringing Laney up with him. "Do you mind feeding her?"

Before Molly knew what was about to happen, Ethan placed the baby in her arms. The soft, warm body cuddled into her and made sucking noises against the little fist.

Two years. Two long years since she'd held a baby in her arms.

Molly thought she would collapse on the spot.

Chapter Three

Ethan found the camper accommodations more than acceptable and was thankful he hadn't been forced to sleep in a frigid barn—though he would have slept there rather than spend the night in Molly's house. After what he'd gone through with Laney's mother, he would never again put himself in a compromising situation. He didn't figure the Lord would approve of him putting Molly in such a questionable spot either.

Shining the flashlight around inside the camper, he found the propane stove and lit it. Molly had said the camper was equipped with electrical outlets, but it was too cold and too late to find the breaker box and make the connections. He opted for the camping lantern he found hanging from a peg inside the narrow closet next to the stove. Leaving it lit, he used the blankets to make up the bunk and, satisfied, started back to the house to ask another favor.

Stomping over the ice-packed ground to keep his footing, he came around the side of the house and onto the porch. Through the window, he could see Molly sitting by the fireplace, holding Laney. Firelight played through her barely red hair and cast a halo around her. Her face was pale, sending her spattering of freckles into relief. And though her eyes drooped with fatigue, she kept them trained on the now-sleeping baby.

Giving a soft knock of warning, he turned the knob, found the door unlocked, and stepped in.

Molly looked up, her relieved expression all out of proportion to his short absence. Did she dislike kids that much?

"You shouldn't leave your door unlocked." He wiped his feet on the rug and watched with dismay as ice fell from his clothes to the polished wood floor and quickly formed more puddles.

Molly stood and came toward him, moving with careful ease so as not wake

Laney. "Who do you think would be out in this storm?"

"Me."

"Yeah, well, you're not dangerous."

"How do you know?"

Her soft laugh raised the hairs on his arms. "Because you're so tired you're about to fall over."

As Ethan took his daughter, Molly stretched and rubbed her arms as if they ached. Warmth crept into him that had nothing at all to do with the pleasant fire and comfortable house. "You didn't have to hold her all that time. Once she's eaten, she sleeps like the dead."

Molly's skin faded to white. Her eyes grew round. "She's fine. I promise. Nothing happened to her."

"I can see that," he said gently. What was that all about? He thought Molly's behavior was odd but blamed it on fatigue. "I seem to be melting all over your living room again."

"I can clean the floor in the morning." She yawned and shook her head. Her shoulders drooped with weariness. "Is the camper going to work out okay?"

"I'm so tired it looks like the Waldorf to me."

In preparation for the trek out to the camper, Ethan wrapped Laney in a pile of soft blankets. With a whimper, she squirmed and made sucking motions with her mouth.

Both adults stilled, waited for her to settle again, before Ethan continued. "I guess I'll say goodnight then. And thanks for all you've done."

He had considered asking Molly to keep the baby in the house for the night, but her nervousness around his daughter had changed his mind.

Molly McCreight had done enough.

"If you need anything before morning, just come on in. I'll leave the back door unlocked."

Even under the extraordinary circumstances, he was moved and heartened by the trusting gesture. Molly McCreight was a fascinating woman, and somehow he'd find a way to repay her kindness.

Exhausted as she was, Molly thought she'd fall asleep the minute her head hit the pillow. Instead, she lay awake for hours, listening to sleet rake the window panes and thinking about Ethan Hunter. Tomorrow, somehow, someway, she had to get him away from her house. Not that she didn't like him. That was the trouble. She not only liked him, she admired a man who would go to such extremes to help someone in need.

But Ethan had a baby and spending those hours tonight with her had taken an incredible toll. Hunger for a child coupled with the fear of losing her clawed at Molly's tenuous control.

A gust of wind rattled the house, howling. Molly sat up. Was that Laney crying? Would Ethan, tired as he was, hear her if she choked? Would he know if she needed him during the long, cold night?

She shook her head, rueful. She must be crazy to think she could hear Laney. Though the camper was near the house, it was too far and the storm too fierce for her to hear anything.

Fear was a tormenting bedfellow.

Samson stirred from his usual spot at the end of the bed and tramped up to stare at her with yellow, curious eyes as if to say, "Will you let me get some rest here?"

She lifted the cover, inviting him under as a peace offering. "Go on. I'll be still, I promise."

As the cat curled, warm and soft, next to

her feet, Molly hoped she could keep that promise.

Forcing herself to lie down again, Molly pulled the pillow around her ears and began to pray, blocking out every obsessive thought.

When she opened her eyes again daylight streamed through the window, glistening painfully bright on the crystal kingdom outside. She heard someone moving around in her house, and the memory of last night came flooding back.

Quickly dressing, she shoved her feet into fuzzy slippers and her hair into a rubber band before hurrying into the kitchen. There she found Ethan warming a baby bottle in her microwave.

Wearing a smile that lit his eyes and accented the interesting scar over his eyebrow, Ethan turned to her. “I hope we didn’t disturb you.”

Stretching, she asked, “What time is it? I thought we’d all sleep half the day.”

“A little after nine.” With a wry grin he nodded at the baby cradled in one elbow. “She shows me no mercy. We’ve been up since six.”

“Six!” She recoiled in mock horror. “That’s obscene.”

He laughed. "I try to tell her that, but she's a female. Has a mind of her own." Balancing the bottle with his chin, he said, "I hope you don't mind that I came inside. I didn't want to disturb you, but Laney insisted on breakfast."

"I told you last night to come in if you needed anything."

He nudged his chin toward the coffee-maker. "I made coffee. Care for a cup?"

With a mock groan, she said, "Ethan, you are my hero."

She'd made the joke without thinking, but she was right. He was a hero. "You sit down and take care of Laney, I'll get my own coffee. And once I'm fully conscious I'll make breakfast."

Settling onto one of Aunt Patsy's old chrome-backed chairs with decided grace considering he held a baby with one hand and a bottle in the other, Ethan said, "You don't need to do that. The coffee is enough."

She leaned against the butcher-block counter and poured a cup of the fragrant brew. With the first sip, she sighed with pleasure and said, "People have to eat."

Serious blue eyes captured hers. "How much do I owe you for all this? The food, the babysitting, the hotel room."

"Don't insult me with money. People help people. This was the right thing to do." Placing her mug on the counter with a thud, she opened the refrigerator and removed eggs and milk. The sooner he was fed, the sooner he'd be gone. "Will pancakes do?"

"Pancakes sound awesome." He lifted the baby onto one shoulder and patted her back.

Milk in one hand, eggs in the other, Molly stared at the sweet picture of father and daughter. Ethan stopped patting, and Molly realized he was watching her, curiosity in his gaze.

She whirled back to the counter, dumped flour and sugar into a bowl, cracked two eggs, and stirred in enough milk to make a nice batter. All the while, she felt Ethan's eyes boring into her back.

"Have you checked the weather outside yet?" she asked when she could bear the silence no longer.

"The sleet has stopped and the wind isn't as stiff, but snow started falling right after I got up. Snow will be treacherous on top of this layer of ice."

"I haven't seen a storm this bad in several years."

She set the cast-iron skillet on the stove

and in minutes, the sizzle and scent of hot pancakes filled the kitchen.

"I ran into a storm like this a few years ago when I was still flying. Grounded us for nearly twenty-four hours."

Molly turned, surprised and intrigued. "You're a pilot?"

"Was. I piloted medi-flight helicopters out of Tulsa."

She paused, spatula in the air, and frowned in thought. "Are those the medical helicopters that carry emergency patients to big hospitals?"

He tipped his head in agreement. "You know your helicopters."

"Hey, I watch reality TV, too," she teased. "You guys are amazing. Did you like it?"

An odd expression came and went on Ethan's handsome face, but he teased in return. "Reality TV? Or flying?"

It was impossible not to like Ethan Hunter. "Flying, silly."

"Flying's the best. I love it."

"Now I see why the company sent you to deliver Chester's medication." Turning to flip the pancakes, she spoke over one shoulder. "If you love flying so much, why did you stop?"

He hitched his chin toward the baby asleep on his shoulder. "Laney. The hours were too erratic for a single dad."

Though she wanted to know, Molly didn't think this was a good time to ask about Laney's mother. From his reaction last night the subject was taboo.

She set a plate of steaming pancakes on the table in front of him and turned back to the stove. "Do you think you'll ever go back to flying?"

"I don't know. Laney comes first now. After the Lord, of course."

He got up, carried the baby into the living room to the makeshift bed on the couch and returned to his pancakes. Molly refilled his coffee cup. Then the hot skillet hissed and sizzled as she poured in more batter.

"Do you live in this area?" She hadn't seen him around, but she didn't socialize as much as she once had.

A forkfull of syrupy pancake paused in front of his mouth. "I moved into Winding Stair about a month ago. UPS offered a transfer and a raise if I'd drive the area out of Mena. So I came down here from Tulsa and checked out the housing, the churches and the child care in a couple of the towns around."

"And Winding Stair filled the bill for all three?" That surprised her, given the housing shortage in the area. Scooping her pancakes onto a plate, she came to sit across the table from him.

"Winding Stair Chapel felt like home the first time I walked into a service. The people there are so friendly. They helped me find a small apartment and introduced me to the lady who owns the daycare."

A stab of longing sliced through Molly.

Winding Stair Chapel. Her church. Or it had been before Zack's death.

She gulped a buttery bite of pancake, felt the lump stick in her throat, and washed it down with coffee.

As much as she liked Ethan Hunter, she couldn't wait for him to leave. His presence—and that of his daughter—stirred up too many painful memories. Once he was gone, she'd never have to think about him or see him again, and that was best for all of them.

A baby's scream ripped through the house. Molly jumped so hard, she dropped her fork and knocked over the syrup.

"Hey, are you okay?" Ethan righted the syrup and laid a hand over hers. "You're shaking."

Ethan's hand felt much better than she wanted it to. Reluctantly, she drew away. "She startled me."

"Cry of the banshee. That's what I call it when she wails like that. The first time I heard her, she scared me silly, but that particular cry usually means she's wet."

While Ethan took care of his daughter, Molly cleared the table and filled the sink with hot water. He must think she was crazy the way she behaved around an innocent baby, but there was no way she'd tell him about Zack.

She was down to washing the skillet when, without warning, the lights flickered once, twice and then went out.

"Oh, no." Although she'd been expecting to lose power, she was still dismayed. She could manage without lights, and the old house had propane heat, but the well pump was electric.

Ethan reappeared in the kitchen, holding Laney. "That's not good."

"Not good at all. No power, no water."

"It would be better if you didn't stay out here." He shifted Laney to his shoulder, holding her there with one hand. "Is there someone in town you can stay with?"

"My aunt tried to get me to stay with her yesterday."

"Great. After driving up that mountain last night, I think I could manage Mount Everest. If you're agreeable, I'll drive the three of us into town in your car. The company can send for the van when the roads clear."

"Sounds like a good plan. My car is in the detached garage next to the camper if you want to warm it up." The trip on flat ground would prove much easier than the one he'd made last night. "But there will be four of us."

At his raised eyebrow, she said, "My cat." If she was holding the cat carrier, she wouldn't have to hold the baby.

"Right. Gather up the cat and whatever else you need while I go out and start the engine."

Ethan placed his daughter on the couch again, shoved his feet into his boots, shrugged into his coat, and disappeared out the back door.

Molly's tension eased as she went into the bedroom to pack. Soon she'd be in Aunt Patsy's cozy apartment at the Senior Citizens' Housing Project, sipping raspberry tea and reliving the last twelve hours. The stress of having an infant in her house would be over. Ethan and his tiny reminder of her greatest pain would be gone.

Bag packed and zipped, she carried the suitcase to the back door just as Ethan stomped through it. Cold emanated from him. He did not look happy.

Shivering against the sudden draft of frigid air, Molly reached behind him to push the door closed. "Is something wrong?"

Blowing out a frustrated breath, he pulled the stocking cap from his head. "Bad news. The power line over the garage snapped."

"No wonder the power is gone. That line feeds the breaker box to the entire house."

"Worse than that." He unzipped his coat as if he planned to remove it. "The garage and everything in it is electrified—a death trap until that line is repaired."

"Oh, no." Apprehension crept up her spine. He had to leave. He had to take that baby out of her house.

"Sorry." His mouth turned grim as he said the words Molly dreaded. "But none of us is going anywhere today—or maybe for a lot longer."

Chapter Four

"I could try walking into town," Ethan said. Given the expression on Molly's face he thought maybe he should at least try.

"Don't be silly. You nearly froze last night. We're safe and snug here so we'll make do until things begin to thaw out in a day or two." An attractive little frown pinched her eyebrows together. "Water will be our primary problem, but there's plenty of that frozen in the yard."

The tightness in his shoulders relaxed. He appreciated her practical attitude even if she wasn't thrilled to have him as a house guest. "Got more buckets? I can start chipping ice."

"The big stock pots are in the storage room. They'll have to do."

"I'll get them. Which way?"

"Back through here." She motioned through the kitchen and down a hallway. "But I can do it."

"That's okay. I might as well learn the lay of the land if I'm going to be here for a while."

Following her directions, he went through the door at the end of the hall only to see more rooms beyond. The old house seemed to ramble on forever. No wonder she didn't heat this section.

He opened the first room, spotted an old table loaded with boxes and assumed he'd found the storage area. He went inside to hunt for the pots.

He found something else instead. Familiar packages. UPS boxes. Most from children's stores. All of them recent additions to the room. All filled with kids' stuff.

"What is all this?" he murmured, gazing around at the surprising contents.

A stack of new sweatshirts and jeans and several pairs of tennis shoes had been transferred from their original packages into a larger box addressed to Hillside Children's Home. Another box appeared to be a work in progress, containing only a handful of toys. Catalogs lay strewn about, open to the kids' pages with certain items circled in red pen.

Either Molly belonged to some sort of charitable group that collected clothes and toys for needy children or she spent a lot of time and money doing the job on her own.

Either option seemed strange to him, considering her reaction to Laney.

What was the truth about Molly and kids?

More curious than ever about his hostess, he left the room to complete his original errand, returning to the kitchen with two stainless steel pots in hand and a lot of unanswered questions in his head.

He found Molly still in the kitchen, except now she stood on a chair rummaging in the upper cabinets.

Holding up the pots, he said, "Found them."

She looked down at him and smiled. "I know I have some candles up here somewhere. Oh, here we go." She handed him a tall pillar. "I was thinking. What about Laney? Do you have everything you need for her?"

"Enough formula and diapers to last a day or two—maybe more." No point worrying about that yet.

She stuck her head back inside the cabinet, muffling her voice. "Then we'll just pray we can get out of here before she runs out."

"God won't let us down. He brought us this far."

Molly closed the cabinet door and turned, frowning. "Are you saying God had something to do with you getting stranded here?"

She started down from her perch and Ethan reached to offer a hand. Her cool skin felt almost as soft as Laney's.

"All I know is that I was meant to deliver that gamma last night."

She took the candles from him. "Because God told you to?"

He shifted uncomfortably. Some of his friends and family rolled their eyes when he tried to explain that still, small voice that spoke from somewhere deep inside him. Would she?

"Not in audible words, no. But somehow, on the inside of me—" he tapped his chest "—I heard Him."

Molly's tea-colored eyes grew thoughtful. "That's true. Sometimes you just know."

Relieved that she understood, Ethan smiled. "Exactly."

Lots of people thought he'd gone goofy since accepting Christ. And sometimes the criticism, the veiled sarcasm, hurt. He'd gone goofy all right, but in a way that filled him with a peace and reassurance he'd searched for all his adult life.

"What about Chester?" she peered inside a lower cabinet, came out with box of matches which she set on the counter. "If you were supposed to give his chemo and you're stuck here, how he is going to get his next dose?"

"By some miracle the Stubbses still had phone service. I contacted my company. They'll make arrangements for a chopper to take him to the hospital for treatments until the roads clear."

He didn't want to think about what might happen if the storm cranked up again. He'd done all he could. The rest was in God's hands.

"I'm glad. The Stubbses are good people." She glanced out the window above the sink. Two parallel lines between her pale brown eyebrows deepened. "What about the broken power line? Are we safe with all those volts bouncing around?"

"As long as we stay away from the

garage." Years of flying low and watching out for electrical lines had taught him to be wary, but Ethan was still amazed that he had heard the sizzling electricity in time. What if he had touched that garage door? He shuddered to think what might have happened. Not just to him, but to Molly.

Which brought him back to her earlier question.

Was being stranded here, on this particular farm, with this particular woman, a part of some divine plan?

Snow fell for the rest of the day, but the sleet and wind seemed, mercifully, to have passed. Regardless of the discomfort of having a stranger—and a baby—in her house, Molly thought the day progressed reasonably well. In truth, Ethan Hunter was easy to be around and his masculine presence was a comfort. The fact that he spoke openly about his faith reassured her in ways she didn't understand or question.

The baby was another matter altogether, but with Ethan present, Laney was in no danger. And Molly would somehow handle the constant fear of a humiliating panic attack.

Together she and Ethan devised a simple plan for making the fuel and food last. Then, while she organized the meals and melted water, Ethan had brought in ice and firewood. He had also checked the sagging, ice-laden power lines around the house and fretted over the huge trees bowing over the porch roof. Most importantly he had not expected her to take care of Laney just because she was a woman. She was particularly grateful for that, though each time he ventured outdoors, she counted the minutes until his return.

After putting the last of the supper dishes away, she wiped her hands on a towel. Heating dishwater on the gas stove gave her a new appreciation of pioneer women.

From the living room she heard Laney's baby voice and Ethan's manly one. He was giving his daughter a sponge bath in front of the fireplace. Hoping for one of those herself later, Molly filled another kettle and placed it on the burner before going into the living room.

The diapered baby lay on a quilt, tiny legs and arms bicycling for all she was worth. Her round face was alive with interest as Ethan, on his knees beside her, carried on a one-sided conversation.

"Are you Daddy's angel girl?" he asked, leaning over her.

Baby Laney cooed in response and slammed one little fist against the side of his face.

Ethan laughed and nuzzled the rounded belly, an action that sent Laney's arms and legs into fast motion.

Suddenly, he scooped the child into his big hands and lifted her overhead, waggling her gently from side to side. Laney's toothless mouth spread wide and a delighted gurgle filled the dimly lit living room.

Molly felt a catch beneath her ribs at the pleasure father and daughter found in one another. There was something beautiful and pure in that kind of love.

Tears pricked at her eyelids. A deep, tearing need took her breath, and she turned back toward the kitchen.

Outside, snow still fell in spits and spurts, skinny flakes that were as much ice as snow. Darkness descended, though the time was not yet six o'clock. Anything that had dared to thaw would soon refreeze.

With no electricity for reading and no TV, the evening with Ethan and his daughter would be a long one. He was a great guy, an attractive man, but he was also a father. Wouldn't he be horrified to know she had been investigated by the police for a baby's death?

The familiar wrench of sadness twisted in her chest.

She stood at the kitchen sink and stared out at the descending night, wishing for what could not be. According to Aunt Patsy she had to stop dwelling on the unchangeable. For a while she had begun to think she had—until the UPS man arrived with his unexpected delivery to remind her of all she'd lost and all she wanted but could never have.

A part of her wondered why the Lord had allowed her nephew's tragic death. And why He had allowed her Christian sister to turn against her.

Shivering, she rubbed her arms and tried to put aside the morbid thoughts. Some questions were unanswerable.

When she returned to the living room, Laney was dressed in red footed pajamas, her face shiny and pink from the bath, and her dark hair neatly smoothed. Cradled in Ethan's arms, eyes wide and earnest, she eagerly sucked down her supper.

A kerosene lantern which Ethan had

carried in from the camper sat on the coffee table and cast a shadowy, golden glow over the man and child. Coupled with the fireplace, it shed an adequate, if dim light.

Molly settled into the easy chair opposite Ethan's, curling her legs beneath her.

"You're a good dad." It was true. She'd rarely seen a man so attuned to his child.

"I'm trying." He slid the empty bottle from the baby's mouth and lifted her against his shoulder for burping. "I made a lot of stupid mistakes before Laney came along. I don't want her to suffer for them."

Molly wondered if Laney's mother was one of those mistakes.

"Everybody has regrets." Recalling the way her mother and sister had turned their backs on her, sadness lay like a rock in her stomach. "Some you never get over."

Gaze steady, he patted Laney's back. "You talking from personal experience?"

She rose and moved to the fireplace, her back to Ethan. Why had she said anything at all? Sure, she was on edge with a baby underfoot, but Aunt Patsy was the only person she ever talked to about Chloe and the loss of baby Zack.

A log burned in two, snapped and fell,

sending a shower of sparks upward like a Roman candle.

"Molly." Ethan's voice was quiet. "Would you like Laney and me to head out to the camper so you can have some peace and quiet?"

No more questions. No prying. Just consideration. How could she be inhospitable to such a man?

This whole situation must be as miserable for Ethan as for her. Stuck here in a stranger's home with an infant to care for, low on formula, no power, and completely out of his comfort zone. And yet, he was cheerful about the entire mess.

Shame spread through her. Neither Ethan nor Laney were to blame for her personal agony. If she were the Christian she claimed to be, she would be thinking of them instead of herself.

"I don't want you to go." Then she blushed at how that sounded. "I mean, I'd enjoy your company if you'd like to stay longer."

He spread his hands wide, lips tilting as he looked around the room. "No TV. No stereo. No computer. We might have to carry on a conversation."

Molly caught the twinkle in his eye and played along. “Could be scary.”

“You could tell me about yourself.”

She tensed, then realized she could talk without revealing too much. “I’m not very fascinating.”

“Let me be the judge of that. Tell me about your job, what you like to do, that sort of thing.”

She curled her legs under her again and sat down. “It’s a rare man that enjoys conversation.”

He laughed. “As I said. No TV.”

“You go first.”

“Cheater.” But he did, telling her about his mother and dad in Tulsa, a married brother in the service in North Carolina, his job and his love of flying. She noticed one glaring omission. He did not mention Laney’s mother.

And in turn, she told him of her short-lived college days, about her crafting hobbies and her job at the senior citizens’ center.

“What about your family?” he asked when she’d told him all she was willing to share.

Molly tensed. “I don’t see them much.”

The answer was abrupt, bringing a tension

into the cozy room that hovered for several beats like a winged creature. Then, as if he knew he'd touched a nerve, Ethan shifted gears. "Tell me about your other hobby. Or is that also a taboo topic?"

"My other hobby? I don't know what you mean."

"I saw the boxes in the back room."

Molly's hand stilled on the rough upholstery. So he'd discovered her penance. She swallowed hard before answering in an intentionally light voice. "Oh, that. I have a soft spot for kids who don't have much."

"That says a lot about you."

Molly didn't want him thinking she was some unselfish saint. She wasn't. Giving to needy kids eased the awful ache inside her.

"No big deal. A little money out of each paycheck. I hardly miss it." She popped up from the chair, eager to change the subject. He was indeed, treading on dangerous ground. "Would you like some popcorn?"

Ethan's blue eyes turned violet in the lamplight. He studied her for a fraction of a second as if he was not fooled by her ploy. Finally, when Molly had grown uncomfortable from the silence, he said, "Is it humanly possible to make popcorn without a microwave?"

Relieved, she grinned. "That remains to be seen."

Ethan laid the wiggling baby on a quilt and stood. "You make popcorn. I'll set out those dominoes you found this afternoon."

"Deal."

By the time the popcorn's buttery scent filled the house, Ethan had rearranged the living room so that two chairs bracketed the coffee table in front of the fireplace. The yellow light from a kerosene lamp tossed shadows onto the walls and ceiling.

Outside the wind howled and the occasional crusted tree limb scraped the windows and siding, but the old farmhouse remained cozy and warm. Molly placed the heaping bowl of popcorn at one end of the rectangular table, and curled into her chair. Samson jumped onto her lap.

"Dumb cat," she said affectionately, resting one hand on his head. "How am I supposed to play dominoes with you in the way?"

"The same way I'll play and hold Laney." Ethan leaned around the baby as he reached for the popcorn. "Very carefully."

The child was propped in his lap, her back resting against his chest. One of his muscular arms wrapped around her middle. Her beautiful dark blue eyes were wide open, staring at Samson in fascination.

"Her radar's trained on my cat."

"I don't think she's ever seen one before." He shoved the popcorn into his mouth, then slid seven dominoes to his side of the table.

Molly did the same, standing the game pieces in two rows for examination. She lifted an eyebrow in his direction. "What? No pets? That's child abuse."

"I never said we didn't have a pet. Just no cat." He thumped a double-five on the table. "Ten points."

Molly made an *X* on the score sheet under his name, then glanced up at him. A little leap of…something stirred in her blood. "Don't tell me there's a poor dog trapped in your apartment with no food and no way to get out if he needs to."

"Nope. No dog."

"I'll take ten myself." She slid a blank-five onto the wooden tabletop and wrote her score on the yellow pad of paper. "What kind of pet do you have then? A boa constrictor?"

An amused smile lit his face and sent the beguiling scar into relief. "What would you say if I said yes?"

She could tell he was teasing. It had been a long time since she'd joked and bantered with a man, and it felt good. "I'd tell you never to invite me to your house."

"Which would be a terrible shame considering that I owe you a return invitation."

"Sorry, I don't do snakes." She heaved an exaggerated sigh and said dramatically, "I guess this is the beginning and the end of our friendship."

Releasing a gusty sigh of his own, he let his shoulders sag in mock resignation. "Okay, you win. I'll get rid of the boa as long as you don't take exception to the shark in the bathtub."

Molly couldn't hold back a giggle. "Ethan, you're crazy."

"That's what Laney tells me all the time." He kissed the top of the baby's head. "Isn't that right, sugar plum? Daddy likes snakes, sharks and goldfish. Dangerous stuff."

"Goldfish?" Molly placed her hands over the cat's ears. "Don't let Samson hear you say that. Fish is his favorite meal."

"That's what the snake and the shark said, too. Poor Goldie."

When Molly tilted back in her chair and laughed, Ethan's eyes danced. Molly's heart lurched in response. Her house guest was not only resourceful and heroic, he was funny and kind and incredibly nice-looking. And his devotion to his daughter was enough to make any unattached woman sit up and take notice.

Bad enough that she had to worry about Laney, but now she couldn't get Ethan out of her mind either. She liked him. And she didn't want to.

It would be better for all of them if the roads were melted in the morning, and Ethan and his baby were out of her life for good.

They weren't.

The next morning the world had refrozen and looked like a crystal kingdom in a fairy tale. All of outdoors wore a thick coat of ice that glistened in the morning sun, every bit as beautiful as diamonds. No matter how inconvenient the ice was, Molly found the sight breathtaking.

Laney lay on a quilt in the living room

making baby noises while Ethan resumed his ice-chipping job. With all the work he'd undertaken, Molly couldn't expect him to carry Laney out in the cold with him. But every few minutes she felt compelled to race the ten feet from the kitchen to the quilt to make sure the child was all right.

She was exhausted, too. She had lain awake half the night worrying about Ethan and Laney out in the old fishing camper. Worrying that they might get cold. Worrying about the unstable electric lines sagging above them. And praying for the temperatures to warm and the roads to clear so they could leave. But the only thing that seemed to be thawing was the food in her freezer. So this morning she was loading meat into baskets to set outside in the winter wonderland.

"Look what I found." Ethan stomped in through the back door, grinning from ear to ear, a portable radio in hand. The intriguing scar lifted over his eyebrow.

Since breakfast he'd been as busy as a politician at election time, doing the odd jobs that no one else ever got around to. He'd repaired the front door, replaced a broken tile in the bathroom, and rummaged around in the barn until he found a tube of caulking to use on the windows. He claimed he was doing all these things in repayment for her hospitality.

Molly laughed ruefully about that one. She wasn't being hospitable by choice.

She piled another package of frozen hamburger into a clothes basket. "Where'd you find that?"

"In one of the camper cabinets." He set it on the dinette table and fiddled with the knobs. Static and a high-pitched *wee-ooh-wee* filled the kitchen.

At the unexpected noise, Laney squealed. Molly jumped and nearly dropped the heavy basket.

Ethan gave her a funny look and said, "She's okay. Cry of the banshee. Remember?"

Molly's throat tightened. She rubbed at it, forcing her windpipe to remain open. "Check on her."

She was behaving like an idiot, but she couldn't help it.

"Okay," he said quietly, and left the radio long enough to retrieve his daughter.

Molly followed him to the doorway, battling the creeping anxiety. Intellectually, she knew Laney was fine. Emotionally, she had to be certain.

Lord, would she

As Ethan bent to pick up Laney, memories of the last two days flickered through his head. When Molly had avoided holding his daughter he'd chalked it up to another woman without a mother's instinct. But that didn't jive with her dedication to the homeless and underprivileged children nor with the woman he'd come to know and like.

Now, understanding clicked into place. In his years as a paramedic he had seen that state of near panic dozens of times. Molly didn't dislike Laney. She was afraid of her. Though he couldn't imagine why anyone would fear an infant, the knowledge made him feel better. It also made him more curious than ever. What had happened to make a grown woman so anxious around an infant?

Whatever it was, he wanted to fix it.

Molly was a good woman with a caring heart. She'd proven that a dozen times since he'd barged into her home and started asking favors. During the long conversations and crazy domino game of last night, he'd come to a startling realization.

Somehow he had to reconcile his baby with Molly. Because he wanted to know her better—a lot better.

The idea shocked him no end. He'd thought he was finished with women forever.

Chapter Five

"You can't go up on that roof. It's too slick and dangerous." Molly's breath puffed white in the frigid morning, and sprigs of shiny red hair peeked from beneath her hooded parka.

"Got to." Ethan rested on his haunches next to the house where he had scraped away enough ice to set up the ladder. "That tree is wrecking your roof. You'll have a leak the size of Lake Erie."

Ever since the storm, he had worried about the many trees surrounding the big old farmhouse. Their strength was sorely taxed by the heavy layer of ice and all were bent into unnatural positions. Last night one had finally given way and collapsed onto the roof.

He and Molly had been engrossed in a serious game of Scrabble when the thundering crash had occurred. He had jumped, awakening Laney, who sent up a startled howl. Molly had screamed and tossed a handful of potato chips sky high. This had insulted the lap cat who yowled and stalked out of the room.

They had ended up laughing until tears blurred their vision and they were breathless. During that moment, he'd stared into Molly's gentle face and found himself wanting to please her, to make her laugh more, and most of all, to chase away the anxiety emanating from her.

Now the small redhead stood in the yard, head tilted back to survey the storm damage. He couldn't help but notice how pretty her pale skin looked in the morning sunlight.

"Do you really think the roof will leak?" Her small teeth gnawed at a peach-colored bottom lip.

"No doubt about it." He secured the ladder and started up. "You could steady this for me, if you don't mind."

Molly hurried to do his bidding and Ethan felt a rush of pleasure. She was a trooper, ready to help, willing to do her part. She not only didn't complain about their situation, she found ways to make it seem like an adventure: board games, lively discussions about religion and politics, creative meals by candle- and lamplight.

A man could get attached to a woman like that. After his mistakes with Twila, he was loath to get involved with any woman ever again, but Molly muddled his thinking.

And muddled thinking always led a man astray.

He squeezed his eyes shut for a moment. He had plenty to do today, and fretting over his past wasn't getting any of it done.

To still the disquieting thoughts, Ethan started up the ladder, his boots clanging against the metal rungs.

Once on the gabled roof, he realized the tree was too large to move in one piece. He would have to saw it apart.

Slip-sliding to the edge, he called down to Molly. "I need that chain saw. Can you hand it up?"

She hefted the tool, then paused and glanced toward the front door. "You think Laney is still asleep?"

"Positive. She naps for a couple of hours at a stretch." He could see his response didn't satisfy, and he continued to puzzle over why a woman who refused to hold his baby worried so much about her. "Why?"

Molly made a twitching motion with one shoulder. "No reason."

She'd had plenty of chances to tell him what troubled her, but every time she'd backed away. Funny how that irked him.

"I can take it from here," he said, reaching for the saw.

Hanging on to the ladder with one hand, she passed the saw up and then surprised him by ascending the remaining rungs. "I want to see what the world looks like from up here."

Being a pilot, Ethan loved the view from above the earth. Nice to know Molly wasn't put off by heights. The fleeting thought drifted through his head that he might offer to take her up in a plane sometime.

Feet wide to maintain balance, he set the saw aside and offered his gloved hand. "Ice is devastating, but beautiful, too. You can see for miles from here."

The safest place on the roof was where the chimney met the long, sloping porch roof. The constant heat had melted a good portion of the ice and the roof was a gentle incline. Situated there, Molly would be relatively safe.

"I have pretty good footing. Let me steady you."

With easy grace Molly made the transition from ladder to overhang and settled into a corner of the eave. "Wow. You were right. This *is* awesome."

Pleased with her wide-eyed response, he hunkered down beside her and pointed. "Look in that big oak. See the woodpecker?"

Molly followed the line of his arm, face brightening. "He's huge."

"The largest of the species. A pileated woodpecker."

"Like Woody?" Her breath puffed small clouds into the frosty morning.

Ethan grinned at her teasing tone. "Hear him?"

The woodpecker's rat-a-tat-tat echoed through the still morning.

"The birds are everywhere today." Her gaze scanned the sparkling ice-coated trees. "See those bright red cardinals? They look so pretty against the white-and-silver ice. And over there, jays and chickadees and a nuthatch."

Ethan didn't bother to look. He was much more interested in watching her face than in watching the birds. Cheeks rosy from the cold and honey-colored eyes alight with interest charmed him. He resisted a totally unacceptable urge to smooth a finger over her soft-looking skin.

"They're probably hungry. The ice is covering up their food source."

Molly turned her head, caught him looking and blushed. He liked the way she did that, just as he liked the smattering of golden freckles across her nose.

"I normally keep seed out for them." She quickly shifted her eyes back to the wildlife. "But I suppose it's covered up, too. We'll have to put out more."

In an effort to turn his attention away from Molly's sparkling eyes and wind-kissed cheeks, Ethan searched the vast horizon below them. Birds flitted about, singing as though the frigid temperatures and frozen landscape wouldn't bring the demise of at least some of their kind.

And then something else caught his eye.

Index finger across his lips, he whispered, "Sit very still and look directly below us, near the edge of the front yard."

A white-tailed deer materialized, a spot of tan suede against the crystal forest.

"Oh!" Molly breathed, gloved hands bracketing her mouth. "A deer."

In seconds a fawn clambered into sight, his slick hooves troublesome on the icy ground. When his front legs went in separate directions, Molly slanted a smile toward Ethan.

Like co-conspirators they sat in hushed silence and watched the deer paw at the ground, digging for dinner.

Ethan had work to do but was reluctant to break the beautiful spell the wildlife—and time with Molly McCreight—created. Who knew sitting on the roof in the frigid morning sun could be so entertaining?

After a bit the doe stopped digging and ambled away. Her fawn followed along, white tail twitching.

"Food is scarce for them, too," Ethan said softly.

"I wish we had some corn. It makes me sad to see them hungry."

That was twice now that she'd said *we* as naturally as if the two of them had been working together forever. The idea felt better than it should have considering his less-than-perfect track record with women.

Even though he'd made those mistakes before he'd turned his life over to Jesus, the consequences remained. And he'd promised to concentrate on raising Laney and to leave the ladies alone.

He just hoped he could keep that promise. Spending time with Molly could become dangerously habit-forming. And until the roads cleared, he had little choice in the matter.

"I'd better get busy," he said more abruptly than he'd intended. "That tree won't saw itself."

"Let me help." She placed a hand on his shoulder and started to rise. Halfway up, her footing gave way on the frosted slope, and she slipped sideways.

Everything happened so fast but to Ethan the whole world stopped. Adrenaline shot into his bloodstream. Without considering the risk to himself, he grabbed for her, caught her around the waist with one hand, and yanked her back, all the while grappling for something to hold on to with his other.

Molly slammed into his chest, and his boots slid out from under him. Together they skidded over the frozen shingles unchecked for several feet.

Fear lifted the hair on his neck as he faced the inevitable. They were going to plummet to the ground below.

Molly wanted to scream but there was no time. She and Ethan picked up speed. Chilled wind pushed at her cheeks. Scenery blurred. Fear of the inevitable fall clogged her throat.

Convinced they would tumble over the edge, she squeezed her eyes tight and gave an inward cry. "Help us."

They came to an abrupt, jarring stop. Other than the sound of their frightened panting, all was silent. Even the birds had hushed.

Molly opened her eyes. They were inches from the edge, but Ethan gripped a vent pipe with one hand and held her with the other. Instead of amazement that she had narrowly escaped serious injury, Molly could only marvel at how strong Ethan must be.

For several frightened seconds they rested on the roof, cold seeping through their jeans, while their ragged breathing slowed to normal.

"That was close," Molly whispered. Her pulse thundered against her temples; she was as unsettled by Ethan's nearness as by the near-accident.

Still clinging to the pipe for support, Ethan sat upright and drew her up beside him. He steadied them both until their position was secure. Molly wondered why he didn't release her.

"I shouldn't have let you come up here," he said. "You could have been hurt."

His naturally tan face was intense and pale and dangerously close.

"I came up under my own power, Ethan."

"But—" he started to argue. Molly placed a gloved hand on his cheek.

"Ethan, it's my roof. You were trying to help me. And thanks to you, neither of us is hurt." She knew she should move away from him, but she didn't want to. She hadn't felt safe in a long time, and Ethan's secure embrace was a haven of comfort and security.

Her hood had come off in the slide and her hair fell across her mouth. As tenderly as he touched Laney, Ethan brushed the lock back from her face.

Something more disturbing than a fall stirred inside Molly. Tenderness was such an alluring quality in a man. Hadn't she admired that characteristic over and over again in his care of Laney? And now he was treating her with the same tenderness.

"I'm glad you're okay." His troubled blue eyes studied her as if he wanted to memorize her face. His warm voice dropped to a murmur. "Very glad."

In that instant Molly thought he might kiss her. As scary as that was, and as long as it had been since she had entertained such a thought, she wanted him to.

He swallowed and tilted his head. From the frozen north a slight wind pushed away the warmth of his breath, bringing with it a new sound. Not a cracking, groaning tree. Not a bird. But a baby's cry.

Molly jerked away and was in danger of going into another slide. Ethan clutched her shoulders. "Easy."

"Laney," she said, almost desperately. Her pulse trembled in her throat. She pressed a hand there to stop the impending anxiety. "We shouldn't have left her."

Ethan cocked his head to one side and listened. "She's awake. Better go see."

As though he hadn't just leaped over her carefully built wall, Ethan moved away to tend his baby.

And as quickly as that, the sweet mood dissipated like the call of the chickadee on the north wind.

During their moments of shared fright, Molly had all but forgotten the insurmountable barrier between them. Now all the reasons for her to stay far away from Ethan Hunter came rushing back in the cry of a tiny baby.

By midmorning of the fifth day, the temperatures hovered around freezing and Molly embraced a ray of hope along with this morning's ray of sunshine that the deep freeze would soon end.

To her relief, after the near-accident and the more disquieting near-kiss, she and her delivery man had returned to friendly banter and cooperative living.

Ethan had to be tired of the tiny, cramped camper, but he never complained. Still, he and Laney were normally in the kitchen for the baby's early bottle by the time Molly awakened each morning. Coffee, boiled the old-fashioned way in a pot from the camper, filled the kitchen with a rich scent.

This particular morning they were arguing.

"According to the radio anything that thaws will refreeze tonight," Ethan said, bouncing Laney on one knee. "So if I'm to have any hope of digging out the van, I need to get moving."

"Even if you succeed, the roads are still treacherous." Molly shoved her hair back, looping it over one ear. Considering she had had no dryer or curlers for nearly a week, she must look a fright.

"I have to try. Laney's running short on formula."

"What if you can't get the van out?" she asked.

"I'll walk to town."

"And leave us ladies out here alone?"

She tried to tease, but the quiver in her voice gave her away.

Ethan's jaw tightened. "I can't carry a baby six miles in this cold."

"I know." Self-loathing dripped inside her as cold and sharp as the icicles hanging outside the kitchen window. Why couldn't she just get over herself? "We'll be fine." She hoped. "But if you have to walk, how will you get back out here? To get us, I mean."

"I'll worry about that after I get to town.

My truck is small and might not make it, but Pastor Cliff has a four-wheel drive." He arched his eyebrows, teasing. "In a pinch, I can commandeer a snow plow."

They both smiled at his silliness.

He was so incredibly brave and she was such a coward.

"Well, you're right. We can't hold out much longer. And you have to be as sick as I am of washing dish towels by hand every day."

Laney had long since used her last diaper and Molly had appropriated soft dish towels and safety pins as replacements. Ethan called her pioneer woman, but the task of melting and boiling ice, washing the towels and hanging them to dry in front of the fireplace had grown tiresome in a hurry.

Elbows on the tabletop, she sipped at her coffee, savoring the strong, hearty brew. Thanks to the supplies she'd bought when the storm was first predicted neither she nor Ethan had wanted for food. But now the most fragile member of their party was running short of formula.

"It's still so cold out there, Ethan."

"Yeah. But I'll be fine as long as I know you girls are safe and snug here." He rubbed at the scar over his eye, a reminder of how stark and white it had looked that first night when he'd almost frozen. She didn't want that to happen again. "Before I take off, I'll bring in another stack of firewood."

Molly pushed aside her empty plate, took one last sip of coffee and stood. "I'll do it. I think there may be another lamp in the cellar. I want to bring that up."

The candles and kerosene were running precariously low and if by some chance she was forced to be alone with Laney after dark, she needed light more than ever.

Before Ethan could insist on going in her place, she threw on a coat and gloves and hurried outside.

Chin tucked into the fleece-lined parka, Molly scooted through the teeth-aching weather to Aunt Patsy's storm cellar. At least here, on the south side of the house, the wind was blocked.

Ice crusts sealed the heavy cellar door. After several minutes of stomping and pounding, they gave way and Molly entered the dim shelter.

At the top of the steps, she shoved aside an old spider web with the elbow of her jacket and hoped a black widow wasn't waiting to seek revenge for the destruction of her home. Inside the cellar proper, she felt along the wall until her eyes adjusted to the darkness.

Winter or summer the old concrete storm shelter smelled the same—like a mixture of gym socks and pickle juice. She wrinkled her nose against the smell.

"There you are." On a shelf lining the far wall sat a green-globed hurricane lamp along with a collection of empty fruit jars, a blue speckled canner, and a pair of dry and withered gardening gloves. An ax and a shovel stood in one corner next to the folding camp chairs and a moldy tent.

She knew people who hated the inside of a storm shelter, but she'd never been one of them. She didn't love the close underground confines, but she wasn't afraid either. There was only one thing that truly frightened Molly McCreight. One irrational fear that controlled her life. And she'd give anything to have a phobia for cellars or crawly creatures, instead of tiny, beautiful babies.

She lifted the lamp down, gave it a gentle shake, and heard with satisfaction the slosh of much-needed kerosene. This was enough to keep her and Laney illuminated until Ethan returned.

As she started to leave Molly realized that Ethan would need the shovel. She took it from the corner and started back up the narrow, sloping stairs.

She was four steps up when the shovel caught on the door's tie-down chain and tipped sideways, knocking the lantern globe askew. Hands full, Molly tried to catch the teetering globe with her shoulder, lost her balance, and stumbled on the falling shovel.

The shovel clattered, the globe shattered and the base of the lamp flew out of her hands. Molly thrust both arms in front her… and crashed down onto the concrete steps and broken glass.

Molly lay prostrate for several stunned seconds. Her hands, knees and shins smarted from contact with the concrete. Her head spun and her stomach churned from the strong odor of lantern fuel spilled all around her. The kerosene's wetness seeped through her sweat pants.

Anxious for fresh air, she pushed off the steps and rushed out of the cellar.

"So much for stocking up on kerosene," she muttered and started back to the house, her errand a failure.

A throbbing pain in her leg was the first

warning that more than her pride was wounded. The bright red blood dripping from her lower leg onto the white ground was the second.

She looked behind her, saw the trail and knew she was in trouble. Between the reek of fuel and the sight of her own blood, she grew woozy.

If only she had a towel or something to staunch the flow.

Once on the porch, she stopped to have a look. A gaping slash cut through her sweats and ran from the side of her calf to above her knee. Several other smaller tears in the pants oozed blood as well.

This was not good. Not good at all.

She pressed her gloved hand against the tide.

Music filtered from inside the house.

"Ethan!" she called, hoping he could hear over the radio.

Immediately, the door opened behind her.

"Need some help with that wood…?" His voice trailed off when she twisted toward him.

"Molly!"

She tried to smile and failed miserably. All the nerve endings running from her calf to her brain had come to vivid life. "I cut my leg."

He dropped down beside her. "Let me see."

"You'll get all bloody."

He grunted an impatient, completely male dismissal and pushed her hands aside. She stared in surprise at her blood-soaked gloves while Ethan ripped the torn sweats up to the knee in order to assess the damage.

"Put your hands right here," he said, guiding her to press hard on the wound. "Looks like you've hit a bleeder."

"No kidding," she murmured, stunned at how the blood kept coming.

"We need to get you inside where I can have a better look."

With no further warning, he scooped her up as if she weighed no more than Laney, kicked the door open, and carried her into the kitchen where he lowered her into a straight-backed chair.

From a drawer, Ethan pulled a handful of towels and fell to his knees before her.

Her clothes stank of kerosene and her head reeled from the smell.

"I stink," she said, embarrassed both by the smell and the attention.

As if she were a troublesome child, he

shot her a silencing glance and then went to work. His expert fingers probed and pushed at the torn flesh.

"This needs sutures," he muttered, his mouth a grim, flat line. "A lot of them."

"Got any on you?" Molly joked, gazing down at the top of his head where she noted, with unusual interest, the way his brown hair grew in a crooked whorl at the crown. The idea that he'd battled a powerful cowlick as a boy made her smile. He'd probably looked adorable.

Busy securing a pressure bandage over the wound, Ethan didn't answer her silly question.

When he finished, Molly tried to stand but was quickly pressed back into the chair. "Stay still. I have the bleeding under control for now, but moving around will exacerbate it."

"My floor—"

He reached for her wrist, felt her pulse. "I'll clean it up."

She favored him with what she considered a coquettish smile. "You're pretty handy, you know that, Mr. Delivery Man?"

A pair of serious blue eyes assessed her. "You're not getting shocky on me, are you?"

Good question. Maybe she was. "My head hurts and I feel a little woozy. I think it's the kerosene on my clothes."

He stepped back. "Better change. Just go very easy on that leg. I'd like the bleeding to be completely stopped before I leave."

"Leave?" She had to focus to remember. Where was it he was going?

He rubbed at the scar, brow wrinkling in concern. "To dig out the van. Remember? The sooner I do that, the quicker we can get you to a doctor."

Oh, yeah. She'd forgotten. Maybe she *was* a little shocky.

Holding to the cabinets, she made her way toward the hall connecting the kitchen with the back of the house. The fat bandage of towels and masking tape made the cut throb more. Wavy lines, whether from fumes or dizziness, appeared before her eyes.

At the doorway, she paused, turning to find Ethan, hands on his thighs, watching her every move.

"I'm sorry," she said.

"For what?"

"Because I'm so much trouble."

His familiar grin replaced the worried

frown. "I'll say you are. First, you try to knock me off the roof, and now you go out and cut yourself just so you can force me out into the cold. I'm starting to wonder if you're trying to get rid of me."

Well, he was certainly right about that.

But he was also completely wrong.

Chapter Six

Tired as he was, Ethan's energy resurged as he eased the van over the frozen earth and right up to Molly's front porch. He'd done it. Armed with a shovel and two bags of kitty litter, courtesy of Molly's cat, he'd dug and pushed and levered until the truck spun its way up out of the ditch. Even in the bitter breeze, he'd grown warm from exertion. Thankfully, the ice had done the same, melting enough from the heat of the tires to set the van free.

All the time he'd worked he had also prayed, thinking of Molly and the vicious laceration she'd sustained. Although he'd tried to downplay the seriousness so she wouldn't worry, the wound needed to be seen by a doctor today. It was deep, down to the fascia, and he'd been afraid to probe too deeply for stray glass and the severed blood vessels. Without equipment, there was little he could do about either.

In her condition, he hadn't wanted to burden her with Laney, but again he'd had little choice. His baby needed formula and Molly needed a doctor. Providing both was his responsibility.

He hoped they'd done all right.

Rapping softly on the front door as a warning, he let himself inside the farmhouse and breathed in the welcome warmth. He liked this house and everything in it, including the owner. Seeing her hurt bothered him a lot.

Right away he spotted his girls in the big blue easy chair. Neither stirred, and with a tired grin, he saw that they both slept.

He paused, recognizing the danger in thinking of Molly as his in any way. Since that day on the roof when he'd fought back the urge to kiss her, he had been forced to recognize a growing affection for his hostess. With his past, he had no right to think of her at all, but he couldn't help it. She occupied his thoughts constantly.

Perhaps it was the situation, being iced in together as though they were the only living beings around. He owed her so much. Maybe his feelings were nothing except gratitude. Since thinking that was the safer road, he took it.

Stepping around in front of the chair, he gazed down at the sleeping pair. Even though her eyes were closed, Molly cradled his daughter securely against her, protectively, almost lovingly.

They looked for all the world like mother and child.

Sadness pinched at him. Thanks to his and Twila's foolish mistakes, Laney would never know this kind of nurturing from a mother. He would be the one to rock and sing to her and to comfort her when the bumps of life came along. He hoped he was enough.

His heart ached with love for the little girl who had changed his life. He would do anything to make up to her for all she wouldn't have.

His gaze drifted to Molly and the bandaged leg. She'd kept the foot up as he'd instructed, but upon closer inspection he saw signs that, while the bleeding had slowed, it had not ceased. All the more reason to stop ruminating and get her into town.

"Molly," he said softly.

Her body jerked and her eyes flew open. She sat bolt upright, Laney gripped against her body.

"Oh, no! I fell asleep."

Her lip quivered and her hands shook in what Ethan thought was a gross overreaction. He took the now-squirming baby from her trembling arms.

"Is she all right?" Molly's voice was frantic.

"Hey, calm down. She's fine." Laney cradled against his shoulder, he crouched down beside the chair. "You're the one with the injury."

"Oh, Ethan." She dropped her face into her hands. "Anything could have had happened. I can't believe I fell asleep."

"Nothing happened, Molly. She's okay." He patted her back as he would have Laney, offering comfort for some terror he didn't understand. "I'm sorry she's so much trouble."

"She's not. She's wonderful. It's just that..." She bit down hard on her bottom lip.

"It's what? Talk to me, Molly. Tell me what's wrong."

"I'm not…good with babies."

He frowned, baffled. She was great with Laney. "What makes you think that?"

"I just do. That's all."

In other words, she didn't want to tell him. And the notion bugged him. How could he fix what he didn't understand?

With a sigh, he levered up and went to pack Laney's diaper bag.

Someday he hoped Molly would trust him enough to tell the truth—whatever that might be.

"Ethan, relax. They'll be in here as soon as they can."

Molly, who sat on the end of an exam table in Winding Stair Hospital's emergency room, didn't know whether to be embarrassed, amused or touched. Ethan paced back and forth between the doorway of the ER and her side. At regular intervals, he disappeared down the hall to the reception desk to make a general nuisance of himself. Meanwhile, Laney slept like a rock in her carrier.

"I don't know what's keeping the doc."

Ethan paused before a diagram of the ear, hands shoved deep in the pockets of his jacket. "Maybe I should go check."

Before Molly could argue that he'd already done that a dozen times, he wheeled on his heel and stalked out the door. She stifled a laugh. No one ever fussed over her.

He'd no more than left when a nurse entered. Molly knew most people in Winding Stair, but this woman was unfamiliar. "That husband of yours is sure worried about you."

Husband? Is that what they thought? "He's not my husband."

"Well, if he's your boyfriend, you better grab on to him. Fellas with those looks and that sweet, concerned nature don't come along every day."

"We're just friends." She hoped they were that, given the time they'd spent together.

The nurse rolled her eyes and reached for a blood pressure cuff to wrap around Molly's upper arm. "Believe that if you will, but I don't think your guy feels that way." She pumped the machine and while waiting for the reading asked, "Running any temp with this?"

"It only happened this morning."

The nurse made a notation on a clipboard and poked a digital thermometer in Molly's ear. "What did you do? Fall on the ice?"

"Something like that." She told the story.

"We've seen tons of ice-related injuries since this storm hit. Broken wrists, hips, you name it. When was your last tetanus shot?"

"Forever. I never get hurt."

"We'll have to take care of that."

Ethan came strolling back in, looking pleased. "Doc's on his way."

"Good. Now, maybe you'll sit down and relax."

He offered an unrepentant grin, wheeled the doctor's exam stool away from the wall and perched on it. "Believe I will."

After her ridiculous reaction to falling asleep with Laney in her lap, she had expected Ethan to dump her at the hospital door and run. Instead, he had hovered as if her well-being was the most important thing in the world. He'd even badgered the nurses into bringing her a cup of coffee because he thought she was cold.

"You sure you don't want me to call your family?" He tilted forward, his strong fingers curled over the edge of the brown vinyl seat.

She shook her head, careful not to splash the warm coffee. "Aunt Patsy is too old to get out on this ice. A fall would be disastrous."

"Isn't there anyone else?"

"Uncle Robert lives in Oklahoma City. The rest wouldn't care."

The chair rollers clattered against pristine tile as he drew closer. "Sure they would. Families always care. Let me give them a call."

Her chest ached at the reminder of how lonely she'd been for family since Zack's death. But neither Mom nor Chloe would come. Mom wanted to keep the peace and Chloe—well, her sister hated her.

It occurred to her then that Ethan must be longing to take his baby and go home, a perfectly natural desire after five days of confinement with a stranger. But out of kindness and an overblown sense of responsibility, he didn't want to leave her alone.

"You don't have to wait with me any longer, Ethan. I know you have other things to do."

"Molly." He took the foam cup from her hand, set it aside, and then wrapped her fingers in his. With the most patient expression, he said, "I've made my phone calls. My job and friends know where I am now, and this won't take that much longer. After all you've done for Laney and me wild horses couldn't tear us away from here. I only asked because I thought you might want a family member instead of a virtual stranger."

To Molly, Ethan was no longer a stranger. Not even close. The admission sent a troublesome warning to her brain.

Just then the door swooshed open and a doctor entered, white lab coat flapping out at the sides. Another nurse, clad in green surgical scrubs, followed. Molly recognized her as the doctor's long-time assistant and smiled a greeting.

Ethan squeezed Molly's hand, then pushed off the stool to greet the newcomers. "Dr. Jamison."

"Ethan, good to see you. How's the class going?"

"Good. I'm learning a lot."

"Let me know if I can help."

"Thanks. I appreciate it. The people here in Winding Stair have been really good to me."

"The way I hear it, it's the other way around."

Molly wondered what the doctor meant by the remark, but before she could ask, he ended the pleasantries and turned his attention her way. "So, what have you done to yourself, Miss Molly?"

Dr. Jamison was the last of a dying breed, a family doctor who knew most of his patients personally. He was not only her physician, he was the McCreight family's doctor, and thus he knew the whole ugly story of Zack's death.

She held her breath, praying he wouldn't say anything in front of Ethan.

The graying doctor pushed up his glasses and bent to examine her injury. "Quite a bandage you have here."

The tension eased out of her. "That's Ethan's doing. He's a paramedic."

Dr. Jamison raised his eyes toward her companion, curious. "I remember someone telling me that. The lab, I think. Didn't you take the gamma up to Chester Stubbs?"

Nothing much happened in Winding Stair without the whole town knowing.

"Yeah, that was me. Did the chopper make it out there?"

"No trouble at all. They flew the Stubbses to Tulsa to ride this thing out. Now, what can you tell me about Molly's accident?"

"She has some loose bleeders," Ethan answered. "I couldn't ascertain their origin, so in lieu of proper supplies, we did the best we could to put pressure on it. The laceration's deep and at least ten centimeters from knee to calf." He spewed out a technical description of the cut, all the while hovering over the table, watching as Dr. Jamison removed the kitchen-towel bandage.

"Hmm. I see what you mean." The wound began to ooze immediately. "We'll have to probe a bit, check for glass or other debris while we seal off those seeping vessels."

Ethan moved up to Molly's side. His face was kind, sympathetic, almost tender.

"It's easier if you don't look."

"You think I'm a coward?" she teased.

But Ethan took the question seriously. "I think you're as brave as they come."

He eased a pillow beneath her head and helped her lean back. All the while, her insides jumped and quivered. Ethan thought she, the biggest coward on the planet, a woman who suffered from anxiety attacks, was brave?

He didn't know her at all.

As the liquid fire of the deadening agent entered Molly's already insulted flesh,

Ethan took her hand. "Squeeze if you need to. This stings a little."

She hissed though her teeth, trying hard not to give in to the pain. He'd called her brave. And even though she knew it wasn't true, she didn't want Ethan to know.

"The worst will be over in a minute," Ethan encouraged. "And afterwards, we'll see if the van can ice skate over to the Rib Crib for dinner. What do you say?"

She concentrated on his words in an effort to blot out the burning anesthetic. "What about Laney's formula?"

"We'll stop by the store first, grab some supplies." He frowned as if in deep thought. "On second thought, let's grab some steaks and take them over to my place. I'll make us dinner."

"I don't know," she hedged. Saying good-bye was already going to be harder than she wanted it to be.

"What?" He asked in mock offense, eyes crinkling in humor. "You don't think I can grill steaks? Why, I'll have you know, Miss Molly McCreight, people come from miles around, from other states, even from outer space to sample my steaks."

She laughed. "Are you trying to feed me or distract me?"

"Both. Is it working?"

"Yeah," she said. "And you're really sweet for making the effort."

He winked down at her, the long scar wrinkling with the movement. "That's me. A sweet guy."

And she realized it was true. Ethan Hunter was a very nice man, kind and brave and thoughtful. He was everything a girl could want.

Nearly an hour later, Ethan carefully pulled the van out of the hospital parking lot. Laney kicked and cooed from her carrier in back, and Molly's cat mewed impatiently from his cage on the floorboard.

Though Ethan was tired to the bone, the idea of an impromptu steak dinner with Molly energized him. He didn't know why. They'd had every meal together for days, but for some reason, he wanted to be the host, to spend time with her on his turf.

"So," he asked, careful to keep his attention on the slick streets. "You still up for my fabulous cooking?"

"Ethan," she started and then paused to

stare out the windshield. Pale, her mouth drooped in exhaustion.

With a sinking feeling Ethan realized he was about to be turned down. To spare them both, he said, "You're worn out. You need to rest."

She touched his sleeve. "Thanks for understanding."

"No problem." But he realized her refusal was a problem. He didn't want to leave her with someone else. Who would look after that wound? Who would make sure she didn't get an infection? "Maybe another time."

She didn't answer and his stomach sank deeper. He liked her. Thought she liked him. Had he been wrong about that?

"Doc Jamison did a nice job on that cut." To everyone's relief, no permanent damage appeared to be done and, if all went well, the cut would heal in a week or two.

"He's a good doctor."

"A good man, too. He teaches the singles' class at church."

"Yeah, I know," she said in a funny, faraway voice.

"You do?"

"I used to attend that class."

"No kidding? I've never seen you there. Why did you stop going?"

She shrugged and he could tell the story, whatever it was, bothered her. "My family attends the Chapel."

Now he was more curious than ever. She wouldn't let him contact her family, and she didn't attend church because they were there. "What's wrong with that?"

"Nothing. I'm glad they go, but my sister and I have some—" she gnawed at her lip, expression stark as she searched for the right word "—unresolved issues. So it's better if I stay away."

He didn't like the sound of that. If not for his parents, he'd have gone nuts during the last year and a half. And though he'd messed up Laney's opportunity to have a strong nuclear family, he was thankful for the extended family that would sustain her. Family was everything.

"Want to talk about it?"

"No." Molly turned her face away and leaned down to tap at the cat carrier on the floor.

He wondered if her family problems had anything to do with her anxiety around Laney? Someday he'd find out. "If you'll tell me your aunt's address, I'll drop you off before I go to the store."

"On Cedar Street in the senior citizens' housing complex."

"I know some folks there. Which one is your aunt?"

"Patsy Bartlett in apartment six."

The name and address were as familiar to him as his own. Patsy Bartlett was one of the many people in this warm and wonderful town who had taken a single father under their wings.

"I know her. She's a great lady. More outspoken than anybody I've ever met."

"That's my great-aunt Patsy. If you don't want the truth, don't ask her."

"Well, how about that? You and Miss Patsy are related."

The fact that Ethan knew her aunt Patsy didn't surprise Molly in the least. Her father's aunt still attended Winding Stair Chapel and had a way of collecting friends from every age bracket and walk of life. Naturally, she would draw Ethan and Laney into her fold.

Though the idea didn't surprise her, it did bother her. In such a short time, she'd gotten to know Ethan Hunter better than she knew most people after months of acquaintance. But their friendship needed to end here, today. With Aunt Patsy in the picture, staying away from Ethan and his daughter might be harder than she'd thought.

Staring out the windshield at the piles of dirty snow and ice pushed to either side of the street, she shifted in the seat, moving her bandaged leg with care.

Ethan glanced her way. "Are you hurting?"

His concern sent that now-familiar warmth drifting through her. She wished she wasn't so susceptible to him. "No. The leg's still numb."

"That won't last much longer."

"I know," she said. But a throbbing leg didn't worry her. The unsteady condition of her emotions did.

Ethan's questions about her family stirred up a much worse kind of pain. And to make matters worse, she yearned to talk to him, to let his cool reason and strong shoulders help her carry the awful load of guilt.

But Laney's happy babble from the back reminded Molly that confiding in Ethan was impossible. Totally impossible.

With heavy heart, she turned her attention back to the restless cat.

In moments, Ethan pulled the van alongside the curb in front of apartment six.

The front door swung open and Aunt Patsy's jolly, apple-cheeked face appeared in the doorway. Molly's mood lightened. Aunt Patsy was a tonic to anyone's wounds, be they physical or emotional. She strained forward in the seat, but from her spot on the opposite side of the van Patsy didn't notice her.

"Ethan Hunter, where have you been?" Aunt Patsy scolded, but the smile on her face said she wasn't the least bit angry. "I've been worried about you."

Ethan gave Molly a wink and shoved the door open with his shoulder.

"I brought you a present," he called as he hopped out and went around to the passenger side.

"Don't think another of your presents is going to get you off the hook this time, young man. Where's that baby?"

"Right here, Miss Patsy. I'll bring her up first."

Opening the storm door a crack, the old lady peered toward the van. "Who's that you got with you?"

"The surprise." Gingerly, he made his

way to the apartment and turned the jabbering Laney over to Miss Patsy. "Be right back."

Patsy disappeared inside the apartment and returned to the door empty-handed.

Molly suppressed a giggle at Ethan's game. She couldn't cross the frozen yard on her own, so she sat still and waited for his help.

Sliding a little on the frozen grass, Ethan laughed as he returned to the van. Molly pushed the door open.

"Easy now," he said as he looped an arm around her waist and assisted her to the ground.

With little feeling in one leg, her balance was off and she slid a bit.

"I've got you," he said, blue eyes shining down at her in a way that made her wish it was so.

"Thanks," was all she could manage as they navigated the slick surface.

The minute they rounded the front of the brown van, Miss Patsy recognized her, saw the bandage, and set up a fuss.

"Oh, my darling girl is hurt. What's happened?" She shoved the storm door wide. "Get in this house right now."

"I'm okay, Auntie. Don't fret." Assisted by Ethan's strong arm, Molly hobbled through the door to the small mauve couch and eased down. "Ethan took me to the ER and I'm all patched up now."

"Ethan did?" Patsy bustled around the sofa, pushing pillows behind Molly. "Don't suppose that should surprise me any, the way he looks after folks around here."

Hadn't Dr. Jamison said something similar? As she settled back onto the couch, she looked up at Ethan, curious.

He gave an answering shrug. "Miss Patsy and the other ladies are the ones who do the looking after. I'd starve to death if they didn't feed me once in a while."

Molly could see he was downplaying her aunt's compliment. She gingerly slid both hands under her knee and lifted her wounded leg onto a pillow.

"Nonsense," Patsy said. "A meal now and again is nothing compared with all the handyman jobs he does around here. Last week he fixed my leaky faucet and cleaned out Margie's chimney so she'd quit fretting about the house burning. It's always something around these apartments, and Ethan's Johnny-on-the-spot if we need him. We old people can't do everything we once could."

Molly's esteem for the delivery man, already high, went up another disturbing notch.

"Aunt Patsy, you'll never be old."

"Tell that to my knees." To prove the point, she shuffled to an ancient recliner, grasped the arms, and sat. "My hinges are plum worn out."

"The knees may give you trouble, Miss Patsy, but you've got enough heart to go on forever," Ethan said.

Patsy chuckled and shook her head toward Molly. "See how he goes on? Got all us old hens clucking over him and his chick." She stretched her arms out. "Give me that baby."

Ethan lifted the kicking Laney from her carrier and placed her in the older woman's arms. "We ran out of plastic diapers. She might get you wet."

"Wouldn't be the first time. That one there," she indicated Molly, "did the same when she was a tyke."

"Aunt Patsy!" Molly lifted up, mortified.

"Oh, sorry. Some things shouldn't be told." But the sparkle in her aunt's eye said she wasn't sorry at all. She held Laney to her ample bosom and patted the diapered behind while rocking back and forth. "I've had you on my mind—and on God's mind, too—ever since this weather started. Worst ice storm I've seen in years. I knew something wasn't right out at the farm. No phone. No way of getting out there. And no word from anybody. What happened?"

Between the two of them, Molly and Ethan told the story while Patsy rocked and patted, rocked and patted. Molly envied how natural her aunt was with the child. She had been like that once.

"I don't like to think," Ethan concluded, "what might have happened if Molly hadn't taken us in that night."

Patsy waved the notion away. "I wouldn't expect her to do any less. That's the way she was raised. Take care of your neighbors."

"I would have been in a fix without Ethan, too, Auntie. The electric line across the garage probably would have killed me if Ethan hadn't been there to notice the danger."

Patsy stopped rocking. "I should have known the Lord would work everything out.

And sure enough, he put you two together to look after one another." She resumed rocking. "What a blessing."

For Aunt Patsy, life was that simple. Either something was the Lord's will or it wasn't. Molly wished her faith was as strong and trusting. Instead she constantly wrestled with the "whys" and "what ifs" of life.

Ethan stood and took the now-sleeping baby from Patsy's fleshy arms, placing the infant in her carrier. "Much as I enjoy you ladies' company, Laney and I have to make a grocery run."

Disappointment stirred in Molly, but she refused to acknowledge the emotion, naming it relief instead. He needed to go, she told herself. To take his precious child as far away from her as possible.

Patsy pushed out of her recliner and bent to kiss Laney's forehead before snugging the blankets around her. "You bring that baby back over here anytime she needs a good huggin'."

"Only if you promise to call if you need anything."

"You got a deal." She patted his arm and moved toward the small kitchenette where the scent of stewing chicken filled the air.

"Gotta check on my dinner. You sure you won't stay?"

"Wish I could." He started for the door, then stopped and turned to Molly. The look in his eyes did funny things to her insides. "I can go to the pharmacy and get your prescription filled if you'd like."

She shook her head. "No need. Gary delivers."

For the first time since she'd met him, he seemed uncomfortable. An uneasy feeling crept over her. Why didn't he just go?

"Look, Molly, I—" He hesitated. "I really appreciate all you've done for me and Laney."

"We've been over all that, Ethan. The relationship was symbiotic."

His lips twitched. "Symbiotic or not, I'd like to take you to dinner as repayment."

A knot formed in her stomach. "No repayment necessary."

His gaze traveled to the kitchenette where Patsy banged pot lids, then came back to rest on Molly's face.

"I'd like to see you again," he said, voice quiet.

A lump formed in Molly's throat. She didn't want him to want to see her. The temptation was great, but the danger was even greater.

"I don't think so, Ethan." She spoke as gently as she could but knew the words would sting. They'd shared much. Seeing each other again would be the normal, ordinary thing to do. But regardless of how much she wanted to know him better, nothing in her life was normal anymore.

A spot on her calf began to ache. She leaned up, rubbing at it to avoid Ethan's earnest gaze. "You're nice to ask, but I can't. I…" Her voice trailed off.

She couldn't tell him the truth—that she was afraid to see him again. Afraid of having a panic attack. Afraid of what might happen to Laney.

Afraid of her feelings.

Except for Aunt Patsy's clatter—a clatter that seemed louder than usual—the apartment grew quiet. She picked at the white tape with a fingernail.

Finally, Ethan broke the silence. "Well, it's been an adventure," he said. "Believe it or not, I enjoyed myself."

"Me, too," she admitted. And she had—most of the time.

Looking up, she caught the puzzled hurt

in his blue eyes and hated herself for putting it there. His expression spoke volumes. If she liked him, if she'd enjoyed their time, why wouldn't she see him again?

Because she couldn't risk him ever finding out.

Ethan was barely out of sight when Aunt Patsy shuffled in from the kitchen, dish towel in hand and said, "Why did you turn him down like that, child? He's a nice young man."

"Don't start, Auntie. You know where I stand on the subject. Ethan has a baby. And that's the end of it as far as I'm concerned."

Patsy perched on the edge of the sofa. "Honey, I love you and I've watched you suffer for two years over this. But you have to let go. Give it to God."

Molly squeezed her eyelids together. "I wish I could."

"You can. What happened to our little Zack was a tragedy. You and your sister have to get over it and move on with your lives."

Get over it. If only it was that easy. But the horror was seared into her memory like a brand, too deep to heal.

Irrational. Phobic. Obsessive. Molly knew all the terms, for what little good that did.

"You think I'm neurotic, too."

"I do no such thing," Aunt Patsy breathed, indignant. "You've lived through something awful. Anyone not affected by that is made of ice. But, honey, you can't keep living in fear this way. Fear is the opposite of faith."

Distressed, Molly sank deeper into the couch. She didn't want to be afraid. She didn't want to be alone. But avoiding danger was the only way to keep the panic at bay.

Aunt Patsy didn't understand. She hadn't been the one to find Zack's limp and lifeless body in his crib. She hadn't been suspected by the police and accused by her own family.

"Are you turning against me, too?"

"Never. The way Chloe treated you is terrible and I've told her and your mother so a hundred times. If your daddy was still alive, he'd put a stop to that nonsense. But I'm not thinking of them. I'm thinking of you. You need a life. For two years I've watched you spin your wheels, going nowhere. You're stuck on that terrible day, hiding out with us old people, hiding on the farm, hiding from life."

"I'm not hiding." Not in the way Patsy

meant. Her presence upset her sister. And as the person responsible for Chloe's heartache staying out of sight was the least she could do. And staying away from people, kids in particular, was a matter of preserving her sanity. The fear of a panic attack hung over her every time she ventured out into the community.

"Ethan Hunter is a good man. Some smart woman is going to snatch him up."

"He deserves a good woman." Her heart pinched when she said it. "And Laney deserves to be loved by a woman who can keep her safe."

"Oh, sugar pie," Patsy said wearily, shaking her head. "You're only a danger to your own happiness, never to a baby."

Molly wished that was true. "I'm tired, Aunt Patsy."

"I know you are. In more ways than one." She patted Molly's arm. "I'll let you rest 'til dinner, but just you mark my words. Ethan Hunter is special and he likes you. If he's the man I think he is, he'll be back."

"Won't do any good."

Molly burrowed into the pillow and closed her eyes again. Ethan's handsome face was there to haunt her. She pushed him away. A baby was dead because of her, and regardless of how much she liked Ethan, she couldn't bear to live through that again.

Chapter Seven

Within the next couple of days, the capricious Oklahoma temperature shot up to a balmy forty-seven degrees and ice melted with the speed of the sunlight beaming down upon it. Chunks fell with thuds from branches and eaves.

"Are you sure you want to go back to the farm so soon?" Aunt Patsy asked.

Molly could hardly wait. Every moment in town made her uneasy.

"The Center's going to reopen tomorrow. I need a day at home to get things back in shape before returning to work."

That much was true. But the whole truth rested in the worry that her sister or mother would drop by to check on Aunt Patsy. They had both already called several times. Once Molly had answered. Her sister's frosty tone, ordering her to, "Put Aunt Patsy on the phone," was enough to bring the terrifying tightness into Molly's throat.

One wrong word, one suspicious stare could instigate a panic attack. She had moved to the farm in the first place to avoid the townsfolk's stares and whispers and the inevitable encounters with her sister. The old house was her haven.

To make matters worse, Ethan had called every day to check on her injury. And she'd struggled long and hard to ignore his not-so-subtle hints that he and Laney drop by for a visit. The need to see him again was strong and troubling.

She pulled her coat closed and then hugged her aunt's shoulders. "Thanks for asking Pastor Cliff to drive me out."

"He was glad to do it. He misses you. We all do."

"I'll call you when I get there. Don't worry."

Taking care not to fall on any of the many remaining patches of ice, she headed out the door and climbed into the waiting pickup truck. She hadn't seen her pastor in several months, not since the last time he and his wife had come to the farm, trying to set up a counseling session between Molly and Chloe. They meant well, but she had already tried everything to repair the rift, only to have her sister scream accusations in her face. She understood that. Accepted it. Nothing could fix the wrong she'd done to Chloe. And the panic attack she'd suffered that day had sealed her decision for good.

"How ya doin', Molly?" The young preacher was a blond giant the size of a wrestler but with a gentle nature that was as disarming as it was surprising.

"Good. Yourself and Karen?"

"Great." Beefy hands on the steering wheel, the minister headed the truck down the slushy street. "Karen's already gearing up for the spring bazaar."

"So soon?"

"Not much else to do until this weather settles. You know how she loves making knickknacks." His sky-blue eyes slanted in her direction. "You ought to get involved again, Molly. You're good at that sort of thing, too."

Painfully bright sun reflected off the

melting ice. Molly squinted at it, heaviness centering in her chest.

Yes, she was good at crafts and "knick-knacks" and loved the creation process so much that she and Chloe had once planned to open a shop together. She also missed the social contact. But Chloe was a mainstay for the women's group, her prize-winning quilts and crocheted items in much demand.

"My sister would have a fit."

Cliff slowed and turned off the main road. The truck geared down, working harder on the now-muddy country roads.

"Maybe if you were around every Sunday, Chloe would be forced to adjust, and both of you could get past this stand-off."

"I doubt it." Chloe had made her feelings very clear. Molly was a reminder of all she had lost, the person whose very existence had caused her grief. If Chloe never saw Molly again, it would be too soon.

"Did you know she's been getting counseling?" Pastor Cliff asked. "She and James both."

Other than the tidbits her aunt shared, Molly knew little about her sister these days. "I'm glad. I hope it helps. She's suffered enough."

"They're considering going to a support group that meets down in Mena. A group of people who've each lost a child."

"That's good." Her chest began to hurt. She rubbed the base of her tightening throat, sorry she'd broached the topic in the first place. "Could we talk about something else?"

Pastor Cliff gave her one of his compassionate looks. "Still having the attacks?"

"Not in a while." But she'd come far too close recently to want to take a chance.

"Ethan Hunter said the two of you rode out the storm together."

Molly groaned inwardly. Another difficult subject.

"He stayed in Uncle Robert's camper, the one he takes to Broken Bow Lake every summer." She didn't want any rumors getting started. She had enough of those to deal with. "He's a good guy."

"I think you made an impression on him, too." A grin split his wide face. "He came by the house yesterday afternoon."

Molly wanted to know how Ethan looked, how he was, and what he'd said about her, but didn't ask. Some things were better left alone.

"He told me about the cut on your leg."

"Clumsy me." She patted the sweat pants covering the area. "But it's almost healed now."

"Lucky thing you had a paramedic on hand."

"Aunt Patsy says Ethan's presence was part of God's plan. Do you believe that, Pastor Cliff?"

More than once she'd wondered what she would have done if Ethan had not been there to help her.

"I never argue with Miss Patsy. She is a wise woman."

Molly couldn't deny that, but she still struggled to understand God's hand in all that had happened, not only Ethan's presence during the ice storm, but baby Zack's death. A plan that included such a tragedy didn't make much sense to her.

They rode along in silence for a while, jostling and straining over the patchy ice and red mud until the farm came into sight. The broken tree limb, looking naked and forlorn, lay in the front yard where she and Ethan had left it. Other limbs had given way and lay scattered about. The yard remained frozen with only patches of dead grass visible beneath the shiny ice.

"I really appreciate the ride, Cliff," Molly said as they pulled into her driveway and parked.

"Don't you want to check the house before I leave, make sure everything's in working order?"

She hopped out, eager to be home, to reclaim the relative peace she'd fought so hard for.

"That's okay. The electric company repaired the broken line. If I need anything I'll have my Jeep."

Cliff hesitated. "You sure?"

"Positive. Tell Karen hello for me."

"Come to church Sunday and tell her yourself."

Molly grinned and slammed the door. Pastor Cliff would never give up. It was both an endearing and an exasperating quality.

The truck spun away, mud and water splattering the fenders. Molly waved, then walked carefully across the yard and into the house, eager to get busy. Most of her refrigerated goods would have to be discarded, and laundry was piled high in the basket, so after removing her coat, she set to work.

Deciding to get the laundry started first

and save the more time-consuming clean-ups for later, she went into the utility room and sorted through the stack of clothes. A tiny pink terry-cloth sleeper peeked from beneath the pile.

Lifting out the baby pajamas, she got a funny catch beneath her ribcage. The memory of Laney's warm, sweet scent and soft baby skin rolled through her.

She placed the item in a stack of delicates. Laney needed this, and keeping it would be wrong. She'd have to return it.

Some perverse part of her leaped at the idea.

After filling the washer, she pulled the on knob—and heard a deep, airy gurgling.

Great. Just what she didn't need. With the power off for such a long time, the water pump must have lost its prime.

But as she started out the back door to check, another sound took preeminence. Not gurgling, but humming. The humming of an overworked well pump. One look at the yard told her why. Water stood in small lakes and flowed from beneath the house. Not the gentle trickle of melting ice, but a flood that could only mean one thing:

The water pipes had burst.

With a sinking heart, she rushed to the main valve and shut off the water.

Five phone calls later, she leaned her head against the back of the couch and groaned.

Pipes were burst all over the county. No one was available for weeks.

Dread weighed her down as she accepted the inevitable.

"Well, Samson," she said to the cat who'd trailed her all over the house, curious about her fidgetings. "Looks like you and I are heading back to town."

She'd survived an ice storm. She only hoped she could survive the aftermath.

"Don't you worry, Mrs. Gonzales." Molly squeezed the old woman's cold fingertips. "I'll get someone over to your place to relight the furnace right away. You stay here, have a nice lunch and enjoy yourself until I do."

One of Molly's favorite things about working in the seniors' center was the relief on a client's face when she solved a problem for them.

Since the ice storm there had been plenty of problems to solve. The center had been inundated with calls. In addition to their regular Meals-on-Wheels and other programs, everything from the need for a ride to the doctor to folks out of food and medicine had kept Molly and other staff members hopping. Many of the seniors were only now beginning to brave the cold weather to return to the center for lunch and socialization. Mrs. Gonzales was one of them.

Molly escorted the bird-like lady from her small office to the main recreational and dining area. She liked this large common room, finding it cozy and welcoming despite the size, due in large part to the warm colors and decorations on the walls. At one end, a sectional surrounded a fake fireplace. At the other, a quilting frame awaited the expert fingers of the Quilting Club. Small game tables lined the walls and longer dining tables centered the room.

Molly and Mrs. Gonzales made their way to a table where two other women chatted over hot coffee. One of them, Iris Flowers clunked down her cup and said, "Molly. Just the girl I wanted to see. How in the world did you know Maud Jennings needed groceries?"

"Intuition, I suppose. I called her and she

didn't sound right, so I ran by her house on the way to work."

Phoning clients who hadn't made an appearance at the center was something Molly did on her own, but she believed making that contact, especially with those who lived alone, was important and necessary.

Iris, who wore wild floral prints befitting her name, pursed crimson lips in irritation. "The proud old thing never told a soul she was in trouble."

"Some folks are like that. Don't want to impose, but I was glad to help out." And she was.

The seniors accepted her, never whispered behind her back or made snide remarks. And in return, she gave them her all, sometimes working long after the center closed. She didn't mind. Usually she had nothing but a cat to go home to.

"You're more and more like your Aunt Patsy everyday," Mrs. Gonzales added. "Isn't she, Iris?"

The other two women nodded and beamed looks of approval her way.

Molly hoped the compliment was true. She couldn't imagine a better person to emulate than her great-aunt.

"Thank you, ladies. Now if you'll excuse me, I need to find someone to go out and light Mrs. Gonzales's furnace so the place will be cozy when she gets home."

"Why don't you get that cute UPS man to do it?" Iris said. "He's right handy at such things."

The old ladies giggled like teenagers and Molly laughed with them, though hers was more forced. All the seniors seemed to know that she and Ethan had ridden out the storm together and teased her about him on a regular basis.

"I imagine he's in Mena today making deliveries."

"And then again," Iris said pointedly, giving her glasses a shove. "Maybe he's not."

The ladies giggled as Molly followed the direction of Iris's gaze.

Her heart tumbled to her toenails.

Ethan, carrying a load of packages, pushed through the glass double doors and came toward her.

When he spotted her gaping at him as though she'd never seen such a good-looking sight, he smiled. Her heart tumbled a little farther.

"Close your mouth, Molly," Iris whispered.

Though her mouth wasn't really open, Molly knew she had to get a grip. She took a deep breath and returned his smile.

"Hi," she said and was amazed to sound so natural.

"Hi, yourself." He stopped in front of her and gazed down with the strangest light in his eyes. She stood there like an idiot, mesmerized.

He looked rested and well. And really, really handsome in the brown uniform that set off his brown hair and blue eyes to perfection.

She'd missed him. Had he missed her?

"Yoo-hoo, Molly. Ethan," Iris trilled while two other ladies tittered. "Helloooo."

Ethan broke the magnetic stare long enough to nod in their direction. "Ladies. How y'all doin'?"

"Couldn't be better." The three women beamed. "Isn't that right, Molly?"

Molly decided to ignore their pointed attempts at matchmaking.

"Deliveries for us?" she asked.

"There are more in the van. Must have been a backlog while the roads were so bad."

He seemed in no hurry to move, but Molly knew she had to do something besides stare like a lovesick cow.

"I'll help you unload."

"Great." Ethan grinned as if she'd offered him the grand prize.

Iris's voice intruded, "Don't forget about Mrs. Gonzales's furnace."

"I won't," Molly said and started forward, eager to get away from the well-meaning women.

The delighted chatter of the trio followed them across the room and into Molly's little office. "Sorry about the ladies. They're all hopelessly infatuated with you."

Setting the boxes on the indicated table, he laughed. "Is that a fact?"

"Every one of them. You must stop emptying their mousetraps and unplugging their sinks."

"Can't. I'd starve to death without their cooking."

"You would not." She stuck a hand on one hip, realized she was flirting, and let it drop. "It's nice of you to help them out."

"Symbiotic relationships seem to be an important element in my life." His grin widened as he repeated the word she'd used in describing their time together. "What's wrong with Mrs. Gonzales's furnace?"

"Never mind. I'll handle it."

"Might as well tell me. I'm going to ask her if you don't."

No use fighting it. The man was a born rescuer. "The pilot went out last night."

His eyebrows rose in concern and the white scar rose, too. "She was in a cold house all night?"

"Unfortunately. And on her fixed income she can't afford to pay for something like that. So I told her I'd find someone to re-light it for her."

"Okay. Let's unload the rest of those boxes and head over there."

She liked the sound of that "let's" a little too much. "I can get someone else."

"No need. I can do it in a jiffy. Do you have her key?"

"It's under the flower pot on the front porch."

He thumped the heel of his hand against his forehead. "Doesn't she know that's the first place a thief will look?"

"Yes, but she thinks Freddy might come home while she's gone." Freddy was the son who'd taken off for parts unknown years before and never returned. Mrs. Gonzales refused to give up hope.

They walked out to the van and carried the

rest of the boxes inside. Then while Molly logged in the deliveries on her computer, Ethan moved around the common area greeting the older adults. They all seemed to know him.

Her eyes kept straying from the monitor to watch his long, athletic strides. Once, he disappeared but a few minutes later, she had spotted him again.

Although they had talked on the telephone a few times, she hadn't seen him since he'd brought her home from the ER. She'd forgotten how his presence could fill a room—or at least, she'd tried to forget.

Encountering him now created a problem. She was much happier to see him than she wanted to be.

She typed in the last bar code and swiveled away from the desk and the window that looked out on the common room. Maybe he'd be gone by the time she unpacked the boxes.

"Molly?" His handsome face peered around her office door. "Going with me?"

Her pulse did a happy dance. Not a good sign.

"I'd better stay here."

"I really need you to come along. This

is my first trip to Mrs. Gonzales's. I wouldn't want the neighbors to think I was a burglar and call the police. Besides, I went all the way back to my apartment for my own truck so you could ride with me without making my company angry. You gotta go."

"Oh." She gnawed at her lip.

The pilot had to be lit and Ethan was willing. Only her selfishness stood in the way. Mrs. Gonzales needed this favor badly. With Laney safely at daycare, Molly was in no danger of a panic attack. And they wouldn't be gone long.

"Okay," she said at last. "Let me tell my boss."

"Tell her we'll be back after lunch."

Lunch. She usually ate with the seniors, but a meal with Ethan sounded really good.

What could it possibly hurt?

Thirty minutes later, Molly sat at a round table across from Ethan inside the Caboose, Winding Stair's most popular diner. The scent of apple pie hung in the air like potpourri, and townspeople she'd known all her life filled the long narrow dining room.

Tension knotted Molly's stomach as she

gazed around. She hadn't been here in more than a year.

At the senior's center she felt safe. Here, she was open to the speculative stares and whispers of any and all. Maybe this lunch wasn't such a good idea after all.

"I thought that dog was going to eat my leg off," Ethan said with a laugh as he shook out his napkin.

Mrs. Gonzales's schnauzer had welcomed Molly with a wagging tale and friendly whines, but she'd taken exception when Ethan had begun to dismantle the floor furnace.

"Daisy doesn't bite. She was looking for treats."

"You calling my leg a doggie treat?"

Trying to hide her anxiety, Molly managed a smile. Ethan was good at making her forget. "Isn't that what mailmen are for? Dog treats?"

"See why I have a goldfish?"

"Don't forget the snake and the shark."

The waitress arrived, earrings swaying, order pad at the ready. She took one look at her customers and said, "Well, hello, Molly. Haven't seen you in here in a long time."

Though the woman's tone was friendly,

Molly stiffened. The dread expanded in her chest. "Hi, Debbie. How's the family?"

"Growing. One more kid and we'll have to buy a hotel."

At the mention of kids, Molly's pulse rate rocketed. Her insides trembled, but instead of the expected reference to Zack's death, Debbie pointed her pencil at Ethan and grinned. "Better watch out for this one. He's trouble."

"Is that right?"

"Positive. Just ask Tom. According to my husband, Ethan cheats at every sport known to man, even in the church fellowship hall."

Ethan's lips twitched.

Across the room someone hollered, "Hey, Debbie, I need some coffee."

"Be there in a sec, Willis." She hollered back, and then said to Ethan, "Better get moving. What are you two having today? The special is fried chicken."

"Sounds good. How about you, Molly?"

Molly agreed, though as nervous as she was, she doubted her ability to eat a bite.

Debbie took their order, flipped over their coffee cups and filled them, then whirled away, bantering with customers and refilling cups.

Ethan folded his arms on the tabletop and leaned toward her. "So how have you been? You're not limping anymore so I'm guessing the cut healed just fine."

"All gone except for a long red line. Doc Jamison says it will fade with time."

At the mention of a scar, Ethan's hand moved to the one dissecting his eyebrow. He smoothed his finger over and over the scar. As before, Molly was tempted to ask about the wound that had caused it, but Ethan didn't give her a chance.

"Any progress on the plumbing problem?"

Moving her gaze from the scar to his eyes, she shook her head. The local plumber was still backed up. "Not yet. How are you and Laney doing since the ice storm?"

Ethan's hand paused at his temple, expression tender. The corners of his eyes crinkled. "Laney's awesome."

"Growing, I imagine."

"Like a weed. She had a cold a couple of weeks ago, but that didn't slow her down."

"A cold?" Her voice rose. "Is she all right?"

Ethan's look questioned her. "A cold, Molly. Not the Black Plague. Mrs. Stone brought over some kind of concoction to rub on her chest."

Molly tried to relax, but the worry nagged her. Had Laney caught a cold while in her care? Had she caused the sickness by making Ethan and the baby spend five days in the old camper?

"I've used Mrs. Stone's home remedies," she finally said. "They're usually effective. Did it work?"

"Worked great. Even worked for me."

Molly paused from stirring sugar into her coffee.

As much as she worried about Laney, she worried more about Ethan. He put in long hours in addition to caring for Laney and doing oddjobs for those in need. And there was no one to care for him or Laney if he became ill.

"Were you sick, too?"

"Nah. But the smell of that stuff cleaned out my sinuses anyway."

Captivated by the pure fun in Ethan's blue eyes, Molly laughed. Ethan had that power—to make her relax, to help her forget her worries, to remind her that she was a woman.

Still holding her gaze with his, he rubbed

a finger over the back of her hand and grew serious. "I've missed you."

She'd missed him, too, a troublesome truth.

Fortunately, she was saved from saying anything when a man paused at their table to chat with Ethan about a hunting lease.

In the background, plates clattered, voices rose and fell, and occasional laughter broke out around the long room.

Here were people she'd known all her life. Yet Ethan seemed more comfortable with them than she did. Natural, she supposed, given the cloud of suspicion she'd lived under for so long. Ethan had proven trustworthy. The jury was still out on her.

Throughout lunch, townspeople continued to stop at their table with greetings. Each time she tensed, but no one mentioned Zack. No one stared at her as if she'd done something terrible. By the end of the meal, she had relaxed and was actually enjoying herself.

And then her sister walked through the door.

Chapter Eight

Ethan watched a radical change come over his luncheon partner. One minute she was giggling at something silly he'd said and the next she turned as white as one of Laney's diapers.

"Molly? What's wrong?" He laid his fork aside and looked around the noisy diner. The only difference he noticed was a too-slim woman with short-cropped red hair standing in the entry. He recognized her from church, though theirs was only a passing acquaintance.

Apparently Molly knew her far better than he did.

He was no rocket scientist, but he wasn't stupid either. Though different in style and stature, the familial likeness was striking. Two redheads with the same almond eyes and high cheekbones could only mean one thing.

"Is that your sister?"

Molly nodded, hand at her throat. "Chloe."

Her tone, broken and anxious, touched him. So this was the sister with whom she had "issues."

Curiosity tempered by concern, he asked, "Should we leave?"

But it was too late. The woman spotted them, jerked as if she'd suffered an electric shock and began twisting the straps of a black shoulder bag round and round in her hands.

She stared in disbelief for several long, tense moments before striding toward their table. If she noticed Ethan's presence at all, she didn't acknowledge it. Her wounded gaze bore into Molly.

"What do you think you're doing?" The words hissed out of her mouth like noxious gas escaping a canister.

Molly seemed to shrivel. Hurt and longing hung over her like a darkness. "I'm sorry, Chloe. I didn't know you'd be here."

Ethan leaned back in his chair and

gripped the table's edge, hardly able to take in the bizarre conversation. Since when did Molly, or anyone else for that matter, have to apologize for eating in a public restaurant?

Though he had no idea what was going on, he considered intervening. From the looks of Molly, she was about to collapse.

Before he could, Chloe, her skin as pale as Molly's, spoke again.

"I don't understand why you keep doing this." She stuck out a trembling hand. "See this? Do you realize how upset I get? Even tranquilizers don't help in situations like this."

"Tell me how to make things better, Chloe. What can I do?"

Molly's reply was gentle and so filled with sadness, Ethan could almost see her broken heart. Without another thought, he slid a hand across the table to touch her. Her fingers were as cold as the icicles they'd melted for water.

"My counselor says I have to find a way to resolve things with you if I'm ever to be happy again," Chloe said, her narrow chin tilting in a martyred pose. "But he doesn't understand. Every time I see you, I remember—" Her voice broke. Tears welled in eyes so like Molly's…and yet so different.

"I'm sorry." Molly's voice was barely a whisper. Her knuckles had gone white against her throat. "Please forgive me. Please, Chloe. Forgive me."

"Forgive?" The redhead's lower lip trembled with victimization. "How can I? All I ask is for you to leave me alone, and yet here you are."

Ethan was fast moving from bewildered to annoyed. If this woman didn't back off pretty quick, she'd have someone else to blame for her problems—him.

He caught Molly's gaze, lifted an eyebrow to ask if he should intervene. She gave her head a tiny shake and pushed aside her plate.

"We'll leave now."

She started to rise but Ethan stopped her with a hand on her arm. "No. Sit down and finish your chicken."

"Ethan, please." Huge golden eyes begged him. "Let's go."

If she said *please* one more time he would come unwound. She had no reason to beg him or anyone else. But her anguish disturbed him enough to let her win.

"All right. If you're certain that's what you want."

"It is. Please."

Ethan ground his teeth and barely refrained from cursing, a bad habit he'd thought was long gone.

"Let me take care of the check." Rising, he reached for his wallet and tossed a tip on the table. Reluctant to leave Molly alone, he locked eyes with the vindictive sister and stared hard, signaling as much of a warning as possible without upsetting Molly even more.

Chloe emitted an affronted hiss and hitched her narrow chin.

Ethan couldn't believe this woman. She seemed to believe she had a right to treat her sister with such cruelty.

Molly leaped up and grabbed her coat from the back of the chair. "I'll wait in the truck."

As she brushed past her trembling sister, Molly whispered, "I love you," and Ethan thought either his heart would break or his anger would explode.

He made his way to the cash register, aware of the whispers coming from the other tables, but too concerned about Molly to listen. After settling the bill, he hurried out to the truck.

Once inside, he started the vehicle to ward off the chill and then turned sideways in the seat. "What was that all about?"

Molly still shook like a wet kitten. "Nothing. Just take me back to the center."

He clenched his jaw, fighting off the very real threat of his temper. "No way. This vehicle doesn't move until you talk to me."

He'd had all of her secrets he was willing to take. They'd been strangers before so he hadn't pried, but now he was a friend. And friends helped each other.

Her hand went to her throat again in that anxious action he'd witnessed far too often. "I can't talk about it, Ethan. You'll hate me."

Hate her? She was making less sense than her sister had. But whatever troubled her cut deep and lay like a boulder on her slender shoulders. Having him lash out, too, wasn't the way to help.

Without stopping to think about it, he reached out and pulled her into his arms. She needed comfort. He could give it.

As soon as her forehead touched his shoulder, she broke. All the resolute composure he'd observed during the confrontation with her sister gave way to tortured sobs.

As much as Ethan hated for a woman to

cry, Molly needed this. Heavy-hearted, bewildered and worried, he stroked her silky hair and let her cry herself out.

There had been a time in his own life when he had needed someone this way. Thank God his parents had been there ready to catch him when he'd fallen. From the looks of things, Molly didn't have that safety net.

When the storm of tears passed she tried to pull away, but he held her fast against the damp shoulder of his coat. She required little resistance to keep her there, and he wondered how long it had been since Molly had had a shoulder to cry on.

Holding her was a simple thing to do. And, regardless of the circumstances, he liked having her in his arms. She smelled like the vanilla candles his mother liked so much. He liked them, too, more now than ever.

The foolish thought flitted through his head that he would buy one for his apartment and burn it whenever he wanted to think of Molly.

Disgruntled by such silliness, he shoved the idea away. Right now, something way more serious than Molly's sweet vanilla scent weighed on him.

He needed to know what terrible secret had torn her family apart. And was still tearing her apart.

Gradually, the tremors in her body subsided to occasional jerks and sniffs. When at last she lifted her head, he smoothed the hair back from her tear-streaked face.

"How can I help you fix this if you don't tell me?" His throat was thick with more emotion than he normally wanted to deal with. Molly had that strange effect on him.

Averting her face, she grappled in her coat pocket and came up with a tissue.

"Some things can't be fixed, Ethan." Her voice, too, was wrought with emotion, only hers carried the added layer of sorrow.

"Not true. God can fix anything." Didn't he know from personal experience? "Maybe not in the way we expect, but He can make things right again."

"Chloe won't let Him. Won't even try."

"Why not?"

She lifted puffy, red eyes that tore at his heart and brought the anger surging up inside him again. Somebody needed their heads cracked for this. Two years ago, he'd happily have done the honors. If nothing else his walk with Christ had helped him see the futility in such behavior. It hadn't, unfortunately, taken away his natural inclination to take matters into his own hands.

"I hurt her, Ethan. I wronged her in the most terrible way."

"What did you do that could have been that bad?"

She fell silent for a moment while the hum of the heater filled the space between them with sound and warmth. He could see the war going on inside her. She didn't want to go there, and yet she couldn't escape the memory.

Shoulders hunched, she took a deep breath and exhaled slowly, shakily.

"After today, you're bound to hear about it from someone. It would probably be better if I tell you myself. You'll hear the truth this way."

He narrowed his eyes. The truth? Did the good people of Winding Stair tell lies about Molly? Regardless of the fact that he attended church with her troubled sister, he'd never heard a negative word about Molly.

A car pulled in beside them. A door slammed, and his peripheral vision caught the flash of a plaid jacket. Ethan kept his attention riveted on Molly. No matter how long she stalled, he would wait.

"Talk to me," he said in the same soothing, cajoling tone he'd once used to gather vital information from injured patients.

Molly stared out the fogging window and followed the plaid coat with bleak eyes.

Ethan clicked on the defroster.

As if the switch had also activated her tongue, Molly whispered, "Chloe believes I killed her baby."

The awful words echoed in the moist, heated air for a full minute. Stunned, Ethan fell back against the seat to absorb her meaning. His brain buzzed louder than the humming van motor. He couldn't take it in.

The Molly he knew wouldn't hurt a flea. She fed birds and fretted over strangers, she provided for countless needy kids, and she pampered the elderly. No way she'd ever hurt a child.

"I don't believe you," he said when he'd regained his voice.

"It's true. Anyway that's what Chloe and most of the people around here think."

She looked so small and alone, sitting huddled against the door with her terrible secret hanging heavy between them.

All of his protective instincts screamed to gather her close and block out the ugliness, to be the shield between Molly and the rest of the world. But it wasn't the world that tormented Molly. It was her own guilt and sorrow.

He reached out, tried to pull her back into his arms, but she resisted, scooting away to dig another tissue from the pocket of her beige coat. Red marks spotted her neck where her fingers had squeezed.

He eased back against the driver's door, allowing her the distance she seemed to need. As much as he longed to touch her, he resisted. The shots were hers to call. "What happened?"

A beat passed. Then two. Her breath whooshed out, adding more fog to the windshield.

"Chloe and James wanted an afternoon out, so I offered to babysit for Zack. He was six months old. I loved him so much." She fidgeted with the tissue, picking it apart in tiny pieces. "We played. I fed him and gave him a bath. He smelled so good." She closed her eyes as if remembering. "I can still smell him if I try."

Something inside Ethan twisted. He knew that sweet, special baby scent very well.

"He was fine when I put him in his crib. Sleeping so peacefully. I kissed his soft little cheek and went into the living room." She pressed her fists together in front of her face, shoulders hunched. "If only I hadn't watched that TV show. Maybe if I had looked in on him sooner."

His medical knowledge clicked into place. He knew of only one malady so unexpected and so devastating in perfectly healthy infants.

"SIDS?" he asked quietly. He'd gone out on a couple of those calls in his paramedic days. No call was more shattering.

"That's what the autopsy revealed." She shuddered. "An autopsy, Ethan. I can't bear to think about it."

Neither could he. He blocked the thought and moved into objective medic mode. If he let his emotions have free rein, he wouldn't be any help to her at all.

"SIDS happens, Molly. You didn't cause it."

"But don't you see? That doesn't matter. Fault or not, my sister's baby is dead. She lost the most precious thing in her life."

"But why punish you?"

"I was the adult in charge. I was the one she'd trusted to protect her baby."

What could he say? No amount of argument would change the hideous loss all of Molly's family had suffered. He couldn't begin to imagine how he would feel in the same situation. Laney was his everything. After all he'd been through to keep her, nothing could be worse than losing her.

But regardless of the tragedy, Chloe had no right to vent her anger and bitterness on Molly. Didn't the woman realize that Molly was grief-stricken, too?

"One thing for certain, Molly. Neither you nor your sister can heal until the rift between you is mended." He'd had enough psych classes to know the negative impact of hanging onto guilt and unforgiveness.

"But being around me hurts her, and I don't want her to suffer anymore. She's been through too much already."

And so have you, he wanted to say, but knew the sentiment would be rejected. Instead he said, "Is it like this every time you see her?"

Pale red hair brushed her chin as she nodded. "I've only seen her a few times, mostly by accident. But every time she looks at me with those accusing eyes, and I feel so horribly ashamed, I leave. I do that to her, Ethan. Seeing me breaks my sister's heart."

As Ethan absorbed the heartrending information, some of the things that had puzzled him about Molly began to make sense.

"This is why you're so anxious around Laney, isn't it?"

"I don't want anything to happen to her."

As terrible as it was, understanding this made him feel better. The fear around Laney coupled with the boxes for children's charity had confused him. One minute he'd wondered if she was as self-focused as Twila and the next he hadn't known what to think. Now he knew. It wasn't that Molly didn't care. She cared too much.

His admiration—and sympathy—rose several notches.

"What can I do to help?"

"I don't know."

Neither did he, but he wasn't about to let this go without some serious thought and prayer. She might not have an answer, but Somebody did.

He touched her cheek. "Are you going to be all right?"

"Sure." She straightened her shoulders and sat back in the seat, giving a mirthless, self-conscious laugh. "Sorry. I don't usually cry all over someone nice enough to buy me lunch. You must think I'm an idiot."

That wasn't what he thought at all.

After scrubbing at her face one more time with the tissue, she fastened her seatbelt. "I'd better get back to work."

One hand on the gearshift, Ethan studied her. She looked exhausted. "Wouldn't you rather I take you to Miss Patsy's?"

With a shake of her head, she drew in a deep, quivering breath. "Not necessary. I'm okay. But thanks."

He put the truck in gear, waited while a passing car arched a spray of dirty water against the back window, and then backed out of the parking place. His thoughts swirled with Molly's predicament.

He considered himself a man of action, a fixer. If a faucet leaked, he repaired it. If a patient needed gamma, he delivered it. When Twila had rejected Laney, he'd taken over.

He'd find a way to help Molly, too.

As the truck splashed through melted puddles along the street's edge, more water sprayed onto the windshield. Ethan turned on the wipers, listened to the rhythmic *whoomp-whoomp* for the last few blocks of the trip back to the center as he considered all he'd learned today.

He parked at the curb in front of the long brick building. Leaving the motor running, he turned to Molly.

"Thank you for telling me."

She tried to smile. "Thank you for listening. And for not running away."

"Why would I do that?"

She shrugged and Ethan saw the hurt hanging on her like an oversized shirt. Her family had rejected her. She expected the same from everyone else.

Unbuckling her seatbelt, she reached for the door handle.

"Molly." He was reluctant to let her go. She needed more than a listening ear.

She paused and swiveled her head toward him, amber eyes questioning.

He cleared his throat. "I still owe you that home-cooked steak dinner."

Her face lit up for the briefest of moments, and he thought she would agree. Then as if by some pre-programmed signal all the life went out of her. "I can't, Ethan. Please understand."

Understand what?

"Why not?"

"I don't date."

His gut tightened. "Anybody? Or just me?"

She reached across the seat and touched his sleeve. "Don't think that. You're the… nicest guy I've met in a long time."

His hopes rose. Now he was getting somewhere.

"Then why not come over tomorrow night and let me amaze you with my culinary skills?"

"I like you, Ethan. And if that was all that was involved—" She stopped herself, shook her head and started again. "I don't want to hurt your feelings."

Realization hit him like a fist in the gut.

The wipers thumped the edge of the windshield and vibrated, scraping at the glass gone dry. Ethan let them scrape.

"I get it now," he said, jaw tight enough to break a molar. "You don't date guys like me. A single man with a baby."

A man with baggage. A man with an

unsavory past. A man whose illicit affair had produced a child.

"I don't date, Ethan. Not you. Not anybody. Not ever."

Nobody? A girl as pretty and sweet as Molly didn't date? Ever?

She whirled away and yanked at the door with both hands. Ethan resisted the urge to pull her back and make her explain. Something more than estrangement from her sister troubled Molly. Something that made her reluctant to be with people, and yet she cared deeply for others. Somehow he knew she wasn't telling him everything.

He reached across the seat and pushed the door open, holding it for her.

Without turning to look at him, Molly hopped out and hurried up the water-darkened sidewalk.

Ethan narrowed his eyes and studied the departing figure. The way her shoulders huddled into the neck of her coat. The way her fingers returned time and again to rub at her throat. Yes, something was very much still amiss. He was certain of that. He wasn't sure why it mattered so much to him, but it did.

And he was also certain that he would

not back off until he knew what else troubled pretty Miss Molly McCreight.

Molly spent the weekend fretting over the calamitous lunch with Ethan. Come Monday, the incident still played in her head like a bad movie.

She'd had a good time until Chloe arrived, and then she'd come apart right before Ethan's eyes.

What must he think of her?

A better question might be: Why did she care? He knew the truth about her now. At least part of it. He wouldn't be back and that was the way it had to be.

She couldn't be interested in him, a man with a baby. The risk was too great for all of them.

With a weary sigh, she pulled a file from the metal cabinet. One of the center's regulars who had slipped on the ice and broken an arm was due home from the hospital. Molly wanted to be certain the appropriate services were in place to take care of him during his recuperation.

After a couple of phone calls, she replaced the file and sat staring at her computer screen. A goldfish swam across the blue screensaver and turned her thoughts right back to Ethan.

He probably thought she was a neurotic ninny. Maybe she was. And that was just as well. She'd come close to suffering a panic attack in the diner and closer still when they had discussed baby Zack. She couldn't bear the thought of giving in to the humiliating weakness in front of anyone, especially Ethan.

The all-too-public scene with Chloe must have embarrassed him. So why had he invited her to dinner?

She worried her lip. Probably out of pity.

Not that it mattered. After her breakdown in his truck, she didn't expect ever to hear from him again. And that was as it should be. As it had to be.

At noon, the tantalizing scent of homemade chicken and dumplings drew Molly into the center's dining room. With the ice finally gone, people had returned in droves, eager for the hearty meals and fellowship the center provided. Voices rose and fell around her as she took a tray and found a place in the buffet line.

The long queue of familiar faces stretched almost to the doors, but Molly didn't mind the wait. It was good to see everyone out and about again.

"Hi," a rumbling masculine voice said in her ear.

Whipping around, she gasped. "Ethan, what are you doing here?"

And how can you look so wonderful in an ordinary delivery uniform?

"Came by to have lunch with you."

She hefted the red food tray in front of her like a shield. "I told you I don't date."

He pretended shock, but mischief crinkled the corners of his blue eyes. "Did I say anything about a date? I don't want a date. I want lunch."

Her pulse leaped and pounded like bongo drums gone mad. "Then go to the diner."

She didn't want to be rude, but his presence did strange things to her resolve.

"Can't. I already paid my money." He jerked a thumb toward the cashier. Seniors ate for free or for a nominal amount, but others paid full price.

She gave in, unable to be unkind to someone she liked so much. She put her tray back on the stack. "I have some things to do in the office. I'll eat later."

Ethan reclaimed the tray, handed it to her.

He looked down at her, more serious now. "Come on, Molly, it's only lunch."

The heat of a blush traveled up her neck. How idiotic to assume Ethan still wanted to date someone like her. She took the tray from his strong fingers. He was right. It was only lunch. Everybody had to eat.

So they shared a table that day. And the next and the next until Molly found herself watching the doorway every day at noon. She didn't understand why she couldn't tell him to leave her alone. It was as though she had some perverse need to stay emotionally tied up in knots.

On the days he didn't come, she fought off disappointment with a stern reminder that they were not dating. They were only having lunch.

Some days she almost believed it.

Chapter Nine

"Here, Molly. You finish painting the faces on the animals while I staple the greenery in place."

Aunt Patsy's cheeks glowed rosy red beneath the bright kitchen light as she took up a stapler and set to work with her usual robust energy.

Between the two of them, Molly and her aunt had turned the kitchen into a mini-craft factory in preparation for the church's bazaar, still a couple of months away. For Molly the return to something she loved to do felt good and right.

Dipping the artist's brush into a pot, she painstakingly painted black eyelashes onto a white bunny. "Think we'll have enough door wreaths to meet the demand?"

"Never do. But with your help this year, we should have a hundred." The stapler made clack-snap noises as Aunt Patsy arranged flowers along a preformed circle. "Ethan still coming by to have lunch at the center every day?"

"Not every day." Like today. She'd almost missed lunch waiting for him, which was ridiculous. She knew he often drove too far out of town to get back by noon.

Patsy gestured in the direction of the back door. "That lock's been sticking. Can't always get my key to work. I told Ethan about it at church, and he promised to fix it."

Molly paused, holding the brush above the small plastic rabbit. "When?"

"Tonight."

A little quiver of anticipation mixed with a healthy dose of anxiety raced around in her veins. Seeing Ethan at the center was one thing. Seeing him here was another altogether. "He'll bring Laney."

Patsy pointed the stapler at her. "Now don't get your tail in a twitch, young lady. That baby won't hurt you and you won't hurt her."

"But what if I—" She bit her lip. As much as she longed to see the baby, it was too dangerous.

"Have one of them attacks?" Her aunt set the stapler down with a thump. "Nonsense. You didn't have one all the time you were stuck out there on the farm together."

"But Ethan was there."

"Well, there you are. He'll be here tonight, too." Patsy glanced toward the digital clock on the cookstove. "Any time now."

"Oh, Aunt Patsy." Just what she didn't need, a matchmaking aunt.

"Don't 'Aunt Patsy' me. Ethan is my friend, too. And this is still my house."

Molly knew full well her great-aunt wasn't trying to be cruel. She was trying, in her own no-nonsense manner, to help. What Patsy didn't understand was how much more humiliating a panic attack would be now that she knew, and liked, Ethan so much better.

"I'm being selfish. Forgive me." Molly circled the table to kiss her aunt's wrinkled cheek. "I'll behave."

She hoped she could. Patsy was right. Ethan would be here. Her heart, traitor that it was, leapt at the prospect.

Tenderness emanated from her aunt's gray eyes. She patted Molly's hair. "Everything will be fine. Now hurry up with those before he gets here."

Molly still had a dozen baby animal faces left to paint when Ethan arrived, ushering in the scent of outdoors and filling the house with his masculine presence.

Across the joint living-dining room, his blue eyes found her. "Hi, Molly. What's up?"

"Go on in there and see for yourself," Aunt Patsy said.

From beneath a blanket, Laney kicked and protested, eager to be uncovered. Between the two of them, Ethan and Patsy lifted her free. Her aunt held the chubby baby while Ethan shrugged out of his jacket.

Laney's bright blue eyes, so like her father's, gazed around the apartment. In the nearly three months since Molly had last seen her, she had gained complete control of her brown-capped head and had grown tremendously. When she spotted Molly, her tiny mouth opened in a smile to reveal a pair of bottom teeth.

Molly's arms ached to hold the beautiful little girl, but her chest constricted in a warning that said she had better not chance such a crazy action.

She gripped the top of the kitchen chair. "She's grown so much."

Ethan grinned, tossing his jacket and the baby blankets onto the couch as he came across the living room and into the dining space. He carried Laney under one arm.

"Babies do that, I guess. I can't believe she's six months old already."

Six months. Molly pushed away the reminder of Zack's age and practiced breath control.

God has not given me the spirit of fear.

When she opened her eyes Ethan stood next to her, admiring the craft items spread out on the tabletop.

"Hey, you're good at this."

His praise was wonderful balm. She tried to concentrate on the bunnies instead of the baby. "It's a fun hobby."

"No. I mean, you're *really* good. Not just hobby-good." He shifted Laney's weight so that she perched on his narrow hipbone. "You could open a store."

"Chloe and I actually considered it before—" She stopped, heart pinching. Setting up a shop with her sister had been a dream they'd both shared.

Sympathetic blue eyes studied her. "Just

the same," he said gently. "You ought to give the idea some further thought. People love this kind of stuff."

Aunt Patsy, who had disappeared into the tiny kitchen, returned with a plate of peanut brittle. "We've got at least fifty more of them to make. You any good with a stapler?"

He grinned and snitched a piece of peanut brittle. "I thought I was here to fix a door."

Patsy gently tapped the back of his hand. "Work first. Eat later."

"Slave driver," he said around a bite of the crunchy candy.

"You had supper yet?"

"Nope. Lunch was a drive-by burger over in Mena. I was hoping you would feed me a good supper."

"Spoiled rotten. That's what you are." The twinkle in her eyes conveyed great affection for their guest. From Ethan's reaction, the feeling was mutual.

"It's all your fault. You keep luring me over here with promises of a work-for-food arrangement. Must have been that cardboard sign that did the trick."

Molly laughed along with her aunt. The idea of Ethan and a cardboard sign was too funny.

"I made a casserole," Patsy said. "Lasagna. Molly and I already ate but there's plenty left for you."

Molly snickered. "Imagine that. She made enough for an army."

"And I'm a grateful man." Grinning, he placed Laney in her aunt's outstretched arms. "Show me that door. I'm starving."

In minutes, he was on his knees at the back door, pounding away. Acutely aware that they were separated by only a few feet, Molly dabbed her brush in bright blue paint and created eyes for her bunnies—eyes that looked like Ethan's. She wanted to go in the kitchen, sit on the floor and talk to him in the way they did most days at lunch. They always had so much to discuss. But she didn't want Aunt Patsy getting any more of her ideas.

Spending time with Ethan at lunch in the company of several dozen senior citizens was far different than seeing him elsewhere. Especially when Laney was along.

But tonight, for some reason, seeing the baby didn't stress her as much as she'd feared. There was no tightness in her chest. Her throat was open and she breathed normally.

But that was to be expected, wasn't it? Ethan was here. Aunt Patsy was here. Nothing could happen to Laney with them present.

Aunt Patsy sat at the table bouncing the pink-clad infant on her knee and talking nonsense that had the baby babbling in return.

Molly glanced up and smiled at the charming scene.

"She's a dandy, isn't she?" Patsy asked, shaking a set of measuring spoons.

"Beautiful."

"And healthy as a horse. I never saw a child so perfect. I bet she's never sick, is she, Ethan?"

Screwdriver in hand, Ethan pivoted toward them. "Hardly ever. I've been really lucky in that respect."

"Some babies are sick a lot the first year. But not Laney. Happy and healthy, she is."

Focused on painting the finishing touches on a bow mouth, Molly recognized her aunt's endearing attempts to assuage her fears.

"Ethan's a great dad," she murmured, glancing up at the handsome man tinkering with the back-door lock.

"I heard that." He gave one more twist of the screwdriver, grasped the doorknob and gave it a shake. "There. Done. Safe and secure again."

Aunt Patsy rose, Laney in her arms. "Then you've earned your supper." She started around the table and then paused. Behind the wire-framed glasses she peered at her niece. "Want to hold this perfect little doll while I microwave that lasagna?"

The gentle, loving face of her aunt pleaded with her to try.

Molly longed to please the dear, wonderful woman who had been her mainstay. More than that, she yearned to cradle a baby in her arms again without fear.

The room seemed to hold its breath. She was aware that Ethan hovered in the kitchen doorway, watching. Laying aside her paintbrush, she said, "Let me wash my hands."

Moments later, heart thundering in her ears, she stretched out her arms. Aunt Patsy smiled and handed over the squirming child.

Relishing the feel of the soft, plump little body, Molly carried Laney to the couch and sat down. Her throat was dry and her insides trembled the slightest bit, but she wasn't short of breath. She could do this.

"Hey, princess," she said. "You sure are beautiful."

Laney's chubby arms and legs paddled in response. Expression animated, she stuck her tiny pink tongue between her lips and blew a wet raspberry.

Molly giggled, a sense of freedom and hope swelling inside her like a cleansing wave.

For the first time in two years, she entertained the hope that the panic attacks were behind her, and that she was no longer a danger to children.

"It's getting late," Ethan said, but he made no move to get up. Laney slept face down across his knees. The peanut brittle plate on the coffee table held only crumbs. And Aunt Patsy had long since retired.

He and Molly both had to work tomorrow but Ethan was reluctant to leave. Tonight had been fun. It had also been progress for Molly.

At the sight of her chattering baby talk to his daughter, something had turned over in Ethan's chest. Some nameless emotion that felt so right and good that he wanted to laugh out loud. She hadn't held Laney long, but the fact that she'd held her at all was important, both to her and to him. She needed to know that he trusted her with his child. And he needed to know she cared.

The admission hit him square in the chest.

"I'm glad you came over."

Molly sat with her feet curled beneath her as he'd seen her do so many times at the farm.

"Me, too." The TV flickered, moving from one commercial to another. He had no idea what programs had come and gone in the past two hours. And he didn't care. Talking to Molly, listening to her laugh, sharing his day with her, was far more pleasurable than any television show.

He wasn't lonely. Didn't have time to be, but whenever Molly wasn't around, something seemed to be missing.

Uncomfortable with the notion, he gently lifted his sleeping child from his lap and placed her in the carrier. She stirred, making sucking motions with her mouth. Ethan smiled.

Molly came to stand beside him, smiling, too. "It's cute the way babies do that."

"She must dream about that bottle."

As if she'd heard and understood, Laney's bow mouth curved into a smile.

They stood there for a heartbeat, gazing down at the sleeping infant. "Aunt Patsy says when babies smile in their sleep, they're playing with angels."

Ethan turned his attention to Molly. The top of her head barely reached his shoulders. "Think that's true?"

The corners of her mouth tipped in a smile. "I don't know, but I like the sound of it."

"Me, too." He also liked the curve of her lips and the faint flush of color over her cheekbones. "What do you dream of, Molly?"

He didn't know where the question had come from, but there it was.

She looked surprised, then thoughtful for a millisecond. With a small laugh, she shook her head. "I don't know. Silliness mostly. Things that make no sense. What do you dream about?"

"You." There. He'd said it. And if she wanted to throw it back in his face, fine. He'd been rejected before and lived.

"Oh, Ethan." She laid a small hand on his shirtfront. "What a sweet thing to say, but—"

He stopped the inevitable with fingertips

pressed to her soft mouth. "No buts, Molly. No buts." And then before he could think better of the action, he leaned down, replaced his hand with his mouth and kissed her.

In the next instant she was in his arms, and Ethan's world centered for the first time in a long time. When Molly's arms circled his neck and pulled him closer, something exploded in his chest. This was the moment they had been working toward since that first stormy night when he'd seen the terror and the goodness in her eyes.

After the bad time with Twila he'd set his mind not to take any more chances with women, to concentrate on being a good father and raising his child to the best of his ability.

And yet, here he was, falling for Molly. Falling hard. He didn't know if it was right. Didn't know if he should, considering his tainted history, but it was happening. He wondered if God would approve of a relationship between a decent girl like Molly and a messed-up man like him.

The question had him slowly pulling away from her sweet kiss.

She rested her cheek against his chest and

Ethan was sure she could feel the pounding of his heart. He smoothed the flyaway hair and held her close for the longest time, wondering, worrying.

He didn't want to cause her more trouble than she had already suffered. A good Christian would be unselfish and walk away rather than risk hurting her. A good Christian would concentrate on being a single dad.

Cupping Molly's face, he stared down into a pair of clear, honest, hopeful brown eyes and faced the truth about himself.

He wasn't such a good Christian after all.

Chapter Ten

Wisps of cirrus clouds played peekaboo with the early April sun. A steady wind, blowing in from the south, brought warming temperatures, and Molly was glad to see the harsh winter give way to spring.

She and Ethan had braved the wind for an after-dinner walk in the small courtyard behind his apartment complex. Laney, bundled in a fleece outfit, a purple stocking hat on her head, rode along in her stroller. Big blue eyes, more alert and curious by the day, alternated between the colorful shapes hanging from her stroller and the activity in the courtyard.

Every time she was with Ethan this way, Molly promised herself not to see him again. But then he'd come by or call, and her foolish heart would take control and totally ignore her common sense.

Though still reluctant to call their time together dates, Molly had to admit she felt more than friendship for her handsome delivery man.

"The jonquils are up," she said, rubbing her sweater-covered arms against the slight chill. "I always feel better when I see them. All that yellow, I guess, after the dreary browns of winter."

Ethan, handsome and athletic in a hooded sweatshirt and blue jeans, bent and snapped one off, presenting it to her. "A pretty flower for a pretty lady."

"Flatterer." But she smiled and took the sunny blossom, stroking the velvet smoothness against her cheek.

Since that night when she had held Laney without panic and Ethan had kissed her, Molly's frozen insides had begun to thaw as slowly and surely as the weather. Scary as that felt, it also felt good. Regardless of her sister's animosity and her own guilt, Aunt Patsy and Ethan were right. She needed to move forward.

Somehow she had to get past the fear of

being alone with Laney. She adored the happy little baby. She had even grown brave enough to hold her and play with her and talk to her, though only with Ethan present.

She hadn't had a panic attack in a long time, hoped they were gone for good, but she was still afraid to take the chance. She never wanted Ethan to see how weak and lacking in self-control she really was. And yet she adored Laney, yearned for her as if she were the baby's mother.

The inner battle raged continually until she wondered what to do. Break it off? Keep going though they had no future? Or pray for a miracle to change her fear to faith?

"I talked to the plumber this afternoon," she said to escape her troubled thoughts. "He thinks he can get out to the farm by Thursday."

"That's good, I guess." Ethan's words came out a little doubtfully, hesitantly, as if he wasn't all that thrilled.

"I'll be glad to get home. Aunt Patsy must be tired of having me underfoot."

"You're good company for her." He reached for her hand, his warm, strong fingers wrapping around hers like a glove. "For me, too. I like having you here in town, close by." His mouth kicked up in a grin that made her heart go flip-flop. "To feed me when I'm starving."

She whopped him with the jonquil. "Did anyone ever tell you that you are a bum?"

He dodged, rubbed the spot where the flower had touched him and laughed. "All the time. But a single man's gotta eat."

He was teasing, she knew, because more than half the time he either cooked for her or ordered out. Take tonight. He'd char-coaled burgers for them on the outside grill while she'd whipped together a pan of fudgy brownies in his small efficiency kitchen.

They strolled on, comfortable together, circling the empty swimming pool, crunch-ing over brown leaves that no one had bothered to rake the previous fall.

"Have you thought about Easter?" he asked.

"I've thought about it." He'd tried for weeks to get her to attend Chapel with him.

"You should come. We're doing a sunrise pageant. I'm Pontius Pilate."

"Type-casting?" She grinned. Nothing could be further from the truth.

"It was either Pilate or Judas, the betrayer. I thought I'd look better in a governor's robe than in a hangman's noose."

They both chuckled.

"Come on," he said. "You don't want to miss my acting debut, do you? Say you'll be there."

She wanted to. "I don't know if I'm that brave."

"Sure you are. You just don't want to upset your sister."

"That's true. Ruining her Easter would be pretty selfish of me."

"Ruining yours is pretty selfish of her."

She hadn't thought of it that way.

He paused to retuck a blanket around Laney's kicking legs. Crouched on his haunches in front of the stroller, he glanced up and smiled. Molly's stomach lifted as if she had dived off the high board. "Will you at least think about it?"

How could she refuse? She wanted to make him happy, to spend time with him. She also longed to be with her church family again. "Okay. I'll think about it."

His smile widened. "I feel a victory coming on."

She pointed the jonquil at him. "Don't be so sure of yourself, buster."

"Hey, I convinced you to fly in a plane with me."

"No danger of running into my sister up there," she joked. Ethan's skilled piloting had made the flight fun and safe. She'd seen her beloved Winding Stair Mountain from a whole new perspective. She'd also witnessed Ethan's love of flying and wondered how he'd ever left it.

"Think you'll ever go back to that line of work?"

He hitched one shoulder. "I don't know. Right now, Laney needs a parent more than I need to fly. Don't you, sugar?"

He smacked a kiss on Laney's chin. She rewarded him with a bubbling laugh.

His remark reminded Molly that Laney had another parent, a parent Ethan never mentioned. Since the first time she'd asked about the woman who had given birth to Ethan's daughter and had been rebuffed, Molly had avoided the subject.

"What about Laney's mother? Why didn't she help out so you could go on flying?"

For the space of several seconds Ethan didn't answer. He stared up into the sky he loved with an expression of immense sadness. When he looked at her again, his blue eyes had gone as distant as the wispy clouds.

"Laney's mother is dead."

"Oh, Ethan. How tragic." Stunned and filled with remorse for broaching the sensitive subject, Molly reached to touch him. "What happened?"

He stepped away, rounding to the back of the stroller.

"Does it matter? She's dead. And Laney only has me."

He started off toward the back door of the apartment, pushing the stroller ahead of him.

"Ethan, wait." Though he paused, he didn't turn around. Molly hurried to catch up. When she reached his side, she said, "I didn't mean to pry. Forgive me?"

He softened then and looped an arm around her neck. "Nothing to forgive. Twila is a bad subject. That's all."

A bad subject and one he didn't care to pursue. A subject so painful that he wouldn't share it with her, though she'd shared her deepest hurt with him.

The idea depressed her. She had a sinking feeling that she might be falling for a man who still loved a dead woman named Twila.

Ethan loved church dismissal, that time immediately following worship service when folks milled around the foyer visiting, too full of love and peace to leave.

This Sunday was no different. As he made his way toward the nursery to get Laney, he stopped over and over again to shake hands, to exchange pleasantries, and to share ideas for the upcoming Easter pageant.

He was sorry Molly still refused to come to church with him but he was sure she was weakening on the issue. She was already attending a small home Bible study with him. Any Sunday now, he expected her to jump in his truck, all dressed up and pretty as a sunrise.

Like a family, he thought. Molly and Laney and him, together. The more the idea took root, the better he liked it.

By the time he fetched Laney from the nursery and made his way back to the foyer, the crowd had begun to thin. A few stragglers chatted in small groups. A man in one group, Jesse Slater, called out to him.

"Ethan. Over here."

He liked Jesse Slater and his sweet wife, Lindsey, who ran the Christmas tree farm outside of town. They'd been one of the first couples to welcome him when he'd joined the church at Winding Stair.

Approaching the group, he said, "Hey, Jesse. Lindsey. What's up?"

The silver-eyed Jesse hooked an arm around his pregnant wife. "Lindsey's making a brunch at our house after service on Easter. Wanna come?"

He hesitated. Until Molly made up her mind, he didn't want to make other plans. "I appreciate the invitation. Can I get back to you with an answer after I talk to Molly?"

"Molly?" Lindsey's face lit up. "Do you think there's a chance she might come, too?"

"I'm working on her."

"I didn't know the two of you were dating." She turned to her husband. "Isn't that cool, Jesse? Don't you think they're perfect together?"

Jesse rolled his eyes, though his voice was warm with affection for his wife. "Sorry, Ethan. The woman's a hopeless romantic."

"Don't tease, Jesse," Lindsey said. "Molly's had a rough time. I think it's wonderful that she's starting to date again." She looked toward Ethan. "Tell her that I'd love to have her come to brunch. We'll catch up on old times and I'll try to talk her into making some Christmas crafts for my shop."

"I'll do that." He exchanged nods with Jesse. "Y'all take care."

Hoisting Laney, who grew heavier every day, he headed toward the exit.

Seemingly from out of nowhere, Molly's sister appeared at his side to pluck at his jacket sleeve. Since the confrontation in the diner, Ethan had kept his distance, not wanting to rub salt in the wound. This time he hadn't spotted her in time.

Dressed in black that accentuated her pallor and skinniness, she asked, "Did I hear you say you're still seeing my sister?"

Her tone was incredulous.

"Yes," he said as kindly as he could manage. "As often as she allows."

"If you care anything at all for your baby, you'll stay away from her. She's dangerous."

Given the grief she'd caused Molly, the old Ethan wanted to blast her with his temper. The new Ethan resisted. Anger would only exacerbate the problem.

Taking a deep breath, he prayed inwardly.

Lord, don't let me blow this. It might be my one shot at helping Molly.

"She told me about your son. I'm sorry."

"Really? She told you?" Bitterness dripped from her, stronger than acid. "And you still allow her near your child?"

A tall blond man whom Ethan recognized as Chloe's husband pushed through the crowd and grabbed his wife's arm. "Chloe, don't. Honey, please," he said gently. "Let's go."

She yanked away and stalked off, shoving the glass door open hard enough to attract the stares of other stragglers.

James turned to Ethan, hands spread in a gesture of helplessness. "I hope you won't hold that against her. She's gone through a lot."

"Molly told me. You haven't had it easy either." As a dad he could sympathize as readily with James as with Chloe.

"It's been a trial for the entire family, but Chloe hasn't even begun to heal. Zack's nursery is exactly like it was the day he died. She refuses to let me change a thing." He raked a hand through his thick hair. "She tortures herself with memories and pictures and by teaching the toddler class. I think if we were able to have another child..."

Ethan clapped a sympathetic hand on the

man's shoulder. He wanted to say something. Wanted to have the answer to the man's heartache and felt helpless because he didn't. Only God could fix this.

"I wish I knew what to do," he said. "The situation is killing Molly, too. Except for her aunt, she's lost her whole family."

"I know. She loved Zack. Chloe knows it, too, but she needs someone to blame. Her mother doesn't help any. She's always doted on Chloe too much, even before Zack's death. Now she tiptoes around Chloe, babying her, and making everything worse instead of better. I can't get either of them to see reason. If her dad was still alive, he'd never have stood for any of this."

"Molly told me she was really close to her dad." Ethan stared out toward the parking lot where the bitter woman sat like a stone statue in the front seat of an SUV. "Losing him. And now this. I don't know how she handles it."

James gave him a strange look that Ethan couldn't interpret. "Like the rest of us, I guess. She's just surviving."

"There has to be a solution. Some way to get Molly and Chloe to resolve this stand-off. Neither is going to be happy until they do."

"Is my sister-in-law's happiness important to you?"

"It's starting to be," Ethan admitted.

For the first time a ghost of a smile touched the man's worried brown eyes. "Good. Two years of this is long enough. I love my wife, but I don't know how much more I can take before…"

James's voice trailed off as if he'd revealed too much.

Ethan shifted, bringing a drooping Laney to his shoulder. Something had to give.

"What if I can come up with a plan?" he asked, and then wondered what on earth he was talking about. "Something that will get the two of them at least on speaking terms?"

"Got a miracle in that baby's diaper bag?"

"No. I don't even have an idea yet. But something has to change."

"Well…" James stared blankly into space, the worry lines around his eyes pronounced. "The situation can't get any worse. I'm ready to try just about anything. If you can think of a way to breach this gap between Chloe and Molly, I'll help you."

"Good. It's a deal then. I'll pray about it.

Think on it. And I'll let you know what I come up with."

A flicker of hope played over James's face as the two men shook hands. Then he stepped away and looked toward the parking lot with a weary sigh. "Better get her home. She'll cry all afternoon."

Thinking hard, Ethan watched him go. He'd thought his own troubles were heavy, but there was a man who made his situation look like a picnic. He wondered if Molly knew her sister had been unable to conceive another child? Probably not.

He hoisted Laney's diaper bag over his other shoulder and crossed the parking lot to his Nissan. Maybe it was time she did.

"Pizza delivery man," Ethan called as he slammed out of his truck in front of Molly's farmhouse. The place looked so different with the buds of spring pushing up through the cold ground and tipping the branches of trees recently broken and pruned by nature's ice.

Molly was on her knees in a flower bed, a trowel in one gloved hand. "What are you doing? I thought you were going to church."

"Don't you ever look at a clock? It's way

past noon." He crossed the grass and handed her the pizza. "Take this inside while I get the baby."

She sniffed appreciatively. "Health food. What's the occasion?"

Grinning, he jogged back to the truck and carried Laney inside where Molly was busy setting out plates and soda pop. A stream of afternoon sun shone through the double windows and warmed the kitchen with a golden glow. The scent of pizza made his belly grumble.

"It feels good to be here again," he said. And it did. Funny, how this place had the feel of a family home even though Molly lived here alone.

"I'm glad to be back here myself," Molly answered.

The fireplace lay dormant and all vestiges of the week without power were gone. Otherwise nothing had changed.

Two boxes, packed and ready for the UPS man, waited by the door.

"Business for me?" He perused the addresses, noted they were headed for an orphanage in Colombia. "How do you afford to do this so often?"

She opened a drawer, lifted two forks,

saw him shake his head and pushed them back inside. "I buy a little out of each paycheck. Bargain hunt."

"And do without things yourself?"

She lifted her shoulders. "A gift without sacrifice is not much of a gift."

He was glad she thought so. Because he was going to ask her for a gift. And it would definitely require sacrifice on her part.

Molly came around the table and removed a blanket from Laney's carrier, spread it on the floor, and held out her hands. "Hello, beautiful angel."

Laney practically leaped into Molly's arms. Joy, like a sunburst, went off inside Ethan as he watched the woman who had come to mean so much to him, kiss his child and settle her on the blanket with a colorful toy. It was a simple action, one that normally would draw no attention at all, but given Molly's anxiety around his child, Ethan was ecstatic to see this much progress.

"I can't believe she's already sitting up." As she pulled out a chair to sit down, Molly beamed at Laney. "Next thing you know, she'll be crawling everywhere."

"She's already trying to." Ethan joined

her at the table. “And she gets furious because her bottom won’t follow her arms.”

With fond looks at the infant the two adults dug into the fragrant pizza.

“So,” Molly said as she peeled a chunk of melted mozzarella off the wax paper. “I thought you were running errands this afternoon. Why are you here, plying me with hundreds of my favorite fat grams?”

“I missed you.” That much was true. Being away from her all day was starting to be a problem. “Didn’t you miss me, too?”

She propped her elbows on the table, pizza slice drooping from one hand. “Hellooo. I saw you last night. Remember? Buttered popcorn and Junior Mints at Mena’s movie theater.”

“Seems longer than that.”

“Yeah.” She grew serious for a second, studied her pizza as if the black olives were fly specks. Ethan wondered what was going on inside that complicated head of hers.

“I actually do have an ulterior motive for being here,” he said, placing his half-eaten pizza on a plate. “Finish your food first.”

She paused in midbite. “I don’t like the sound of that.”

“No, you won’t like this conversation, but

we have to have it. I talked to James today after church."

The pizza slice plopped onto her plate. One hand reached reflexively for her throat. "My brother-in-law?"

"Yes. He told me something that might help."

Her eyes grew as large as the flowered plate. "Help with what? Nothing can change the fact that my sister hates me, if that's what you mean."

"I don't think she does, Molly. I think she's angry at God and is afraid of admitting that so she blames you. Did you know she and James haven't been able to conceive another child?"

She closed her eyes, stricken. Her small body seemed to draw into itself. "Oh, that's awful."

"I didn't tell you to make you feel bad. I thought knowing would help you to understand that you aren't the cause of her unhappiness."

"Ethan, her son is dead and now she can't have another child. That makes me feel ten times worse. Not better."

"Look, Molly, you and Chloe have to resolve this issue. It's killing you both."

"I want to. More than anything. But she won't let me."

"Then take steps to change that. Start going to church again. Make her face you, and by doing so, face the problem."

"I can't." Molly's skin paled, and she pushed the pizza plate away. One hand stroked the column of her throat over and over again. "I wish I could, but I just can't."

Torn between exasperation and compassion, Ethan rounded the table and knelt beside her chair. He hated to see her upset. "Hey. It's okay. I understand."

"Do you?"

"Not completely," he answered honestly. "But in a way I do. You feel guilty. And responsible. I know something about that kind of thing myself."

Molly studied him for moment, and then her voice grew gentle. "You're talking about Laney's mother, aren't you?"

His gut knotted. Would she think less of him if she knew the truth?

"Yeah, I am."

His failure with Twila was nothing compared to losing a child, but the two situations related in a way. They both changed the directions of lives and caused a great deal of heartache. He'd wrestled with his own culpability enough to understand how difficult it could be to forgive oneself. In truth, he was still working on it.

Laney's toy banged repeatedly against the floor while Ethan debated the wisdom of telling Molly about his past.

His partying days seemed like another life. Someone else's life. Reliving that time, even in memory, pained and shamed him. But maybe sharing his own struggle would help Molly through hers.

Finally, when the silence between them grew long, Molly brought her hand to rest lightly, comfortingly next to his temple and said, "You can tell me anything, Ethan. I've told you plenty of painful things."

But she had been innocent. He hadn't been.

He drew in a strengthening breath and exhaled in one rushing gust. "I didn't become a Christian until shortly before Laney was born." He grasped her hand and pressed it against his cheek. "That's not an excuse for bad behavior, but I want you to understand that Christ changed me."

"Nobody's life is perfect, Ethan. Even after we accept the Lord."

"True, but I wanted you to know that I've changed. I'm not the kind of man I was back then." He didn't know how much to tell, what to leave out, so finally, he said, "In my family if a guy gets a girl pregnant, he marries her."

To her credit, she didn't pull away, and he understood that she must have long ago guessed this much about Laney's birth. "Some people call that old-fashioned," she said.

"Do you?"

She gazed down at him with gentle eyes. "I call it honorable."

"Twila didn't."

"Did you love her?"

He stifled a smile. Leave it to Molly to go straight to the important stuff.

"I hope you won't think less of me for this, but I doubt if I ever did love her. I never want Laney to know that. She'll never know that. I want her to feel special and wanted every day of her life."

"She will." Molly glanced at the happily babbling baby. "She already does. But what about Twila? Did she love you?"

He shook his head and rose, pulling a chair around so that they sat knee to knee, facing one another.

"Not even close. She was furious when she found out she was pregnant. We had a huge fight." He rubbed at the scar over his eye, remembering the ugliness. "She screamed and cried, said she wasn't going to be saddled with a kid."

"Sad." They both looked at the beautiful child playing on the patchwork quilt. "She threw away the best thing that ever happened to her."

"Laney? Or me?"

Molly turned her head, met his eyes. The corner of her mouth tilted. "Both."

Liking the sound of that, Ethan allowed a smile but quickly sobered again. The subject was far too serious. "Twila didn't agree, and if I hadn't threatened her with every lawsuit known to man—some that don't even exist—Laney would never have been born."

"It must have been a very bad time."

"The worst. But good, too. Getting into that predicament, having to fight for nine long, frightening months to save my child, made me examine my own life. I didn't like what I discovered."

"So you turned to God?"

"Eventually. One of my paramedic coworkers was a Christian. He helped me a lot during those months. I noticed a peace in him that I didn't have. I wanted that. Needed it." He propped an elbow on the table and rubbed at his chin. "Boy, did I need it."

Molly took up a slice of pizza again, turned it around in her fingers and picked disinterestedly at an olive. "What happened to Twila?"

Her eyes flickered to his and then back to the pizza. He could tell she wasn't thinking about food.

"The day after Laney was born she signed over all parental rights, told me I was the world's biggest loser, and went back to her life without me or my baby." He tapped a knuckle against his chin, readied himself for the wave of guilt that was sure to come. "She died in a car wreck five weeks later. Under the influence."

Molly's head snapped up. The pizza thudded to the tabletop. "Ethan!"

"Yeah. She'd been out with our old party gang. The same crowd I had been running with only a few months before."

"You weren't with her?"

"No." He frowned, surprised at the question. Hadn't he just told her that Twila had walked away from him and Laney without a backward glance? "Why would you think that?"

"The scar. A car accident. I just thought…"

He reached up, touched the long white line above his eye.

"No, not then." But he could understand why she would think a car accident had caused such a long, ugly scar. "This was her reaction when I went to her apartment with a court order."

"She cut you?" Molly's eyes grew wide with horror. "On purpose?"

He tried to make a joke of it, though the memory of a knife blade slashing within inches of his eye was anything but funny. "Never make a woman mad when she's slicing tomatoes."

Molly didn't see the humor. "That's hideous. How could she do such a thing?"

"Twila had a lot problems I didn't know anything about at the time. We hadn't dated all that long." Another fact that shamed him. He hadn't really known her as a person, only as a beautiful face and body. "She wasn't a terrible person. Just terribly…lost."

"You did the best you could, Ethan."

"Did I?"

"Under the circumstances, what else could you have done? You couldn't let her abort Laney."

"No. But I wonder if things would have been different if I had been a Christian then. Maybe I could have been a better influence. Maybe I could have helped her instead of making things worse." He sighed, lifting his shoulders in a gesture of helplessness. "But by the time I had started to turn my life around, she was six months along with Laney and would no longer speak to me except to cuss and scream that I was ruining her life."

He heard the regret in his voice and knew that Molly heard it, too. She took one of his hands in hers and rubbed a thumb across the calloused palm. Her need to comfort him brought a smile.

"You're good for me."

"How so?"

"I've been afraid to tell you all this. Afraid you'd think less of me."

Molly returned the smile as she linked her fingers with his. "Everybody has regrets, but you've taken a bad situation and worked hard to make it right."

"And that's what I'm asking you to do, Molly."

"I don't understand." Her face registered confusion.

"Come to the church league basketball game Tuesday night. Take a step toward reconciliation."

She pulled her hand away. "I can't. People at the church don't want me there."

"Sure they do."

She shook her head. "No. They think I did something terrible. They whisper and stare."

"You don't have a problem with the Bible study group. What's the difference?"

"Bible group is four other people. And my sister isn't there to remind everyone of what happened."

"According to Aunt Patsy you haven't been to the chapel since Zack died. Naturally, people were whispering then, but, Molly, no one is talking about you now except to say they miss you."

"Do they really say that?"

"Yeah. Lindsey Slater wants to invite you to Easter brunch. She told me so today."

Fear, longing, indecision all flickered over her face. "I don't know."

Why wouldn't she try? She wanted to. What made her back away every time the issue tried to come to a head?

"Tell you what." He stood and held out both hands to pull her up with him. "Go with me to the ball game. If you feel uncomfortable at all at any point, I'll bring you straight home. Immediately. Just say the word and we're out of there."

Her amber eyes clouded with indecision. She wanted to so badly, he was certain of it, but fear paralyzed her.

"Chloe hates sports. She won't be there," she said, more to herself than to him.

He grasped her chin and tilted her face upward, longing to wipe away the anxiety, to protect her against the demons that tormented her.

"Please. Try. If not for yourself, for me. I'll take care of you."

"Why are you so sweet to me?"

"Why?" He blinked at her, as bewildered by the question as he was by the obvious answer. "I think you know why."

In the next instant, he lowered his lips to hers and kissed her.

She sighed against his mouth, and he tightened his embrace, drawing her as close as he dared. She was fragile, pure and special, and he cherished that about her.

When the kiss ended, she looked at him

with eyes now shining instead of troubled. "You cheat."

He leaned his forehead against hers and laughed softly. "Did it work?"

"Promise you'll bring me right home if anything happens?"

He studied the smooth curve of her cheek, the tiny smattering of golden freckles across her nose, and the full tilt of her lips, troublingly aware that he wanted more than a basketball game from Molly McCreight.

"Promise." His heart thudded with hope as he watched her struggle against self doubt and move toward trusting herself—and him.

"Okay," she whispered. "I'll try."

And the burst of pleasure Ethan experienced was far out of proportion to the victory. She hadn't agreed to meet with Chloe. She hadn't even agreed to go to an actual church service. But Molly was going with him to a church function, and nothing had felt that right in a long time.

Chapter Eleven

Molly's heart pounded so loudly, she could feel the rush of blood through her temples. All afternoon at the center, she'd thought of little except this moment.

Crunching over the graveled parking lot with Ethan at her side, she had to force her legs to keep moving toward the long metal building that housed the Winding Stair Chapel's Fellowship Hall.

"You're gonna be fine," Ethan said, one hand riding gently at the small of her back.

She sucked in a lungful of cool, clean mountain air and nodded, still amazed that he'd talked her into this. And even though she knew he was right, she was scared.

But Ethan knew about being scared. He'd

been scared too. Scared during those long months when Twila wanted to abort his child. Scared of being a single father. Scared he wouldn't measure up. But he'd turned it all over to the Lord and kept putting one foot in front of the other.

Sharing his story with her couldn't have been easy either, but he'd done it to help her. And she could do this to please him.

Hand on the metal doorknob, he looked down at her and winked. "Piece of cake."

"I'm okay."

"It's not you I'm worried about. It's Tom Castor's team. They beat the pants off us last time. I don't want to be humiliated in front of my girl."

His girl? Was she his girl?

The title settled on her like a crown on a princess. Ethan's girl. Whether she was smart to develop a relationship with a single father or not, it was happening.

"Then you better play hard, mister. Tom has the killer instinct."

While Ethan kept her attention with his silly talk of the upcoming game, they entered the rec hall and moved into a group of people. Molly hardly noticed.

A teenage girl she didn't recognize pushed through the crowd. "Hi, Ethan."

Ethan, looking a little uncomfortable, shifted Laney's weight. "How ya doin', Cass?"

"Good. Want me to watch Laney while you play?" The girl held her arms out. The baby strained forward and Ethan let her go.

"She's a handful lately," Ethan said as the transfer was made from his arms to the girl's.

"That's okay. You know I don't mind." Cass's bright smile was more for Ethan than for Laney. "I'm always available to you." She giggled and made calf eyes at Ethan. "As a sitter, I mean. I adore babies. Especially Laney."

Molly fought the urge to grab Laney away from the girl. What was Ethan thinking, allowing a teenager to watch Laney? What if something happened? And why was she so flirty with Ethan? She was just a kid.

"When you get tired of playing with her," Molly heard herself say. "I'll be in the stands. Bring her to me."

She couldn't believe she'd said that. Having someone other than herself look after Laney made perfect sense. But Molly had the possessive desire to keep Laney with her.

Cass shot her a quick, dismissive glance before returning her attention to Ethan. "I'll be cheering for you, Ethan. Have a great game."

"Thanks." Casually, Ethan looped an arm over Molly's shoulders and drew her against his side. "And, like Molly said, bring Laney to her if she gets fussy."

The teenager couldn't miss the implication and Molly felt foolishly vindicated.

"Sure. Whatever." The girl walked away, toting Laney on one hip.

"She has a crush on you." *Not that I blame her, though. I am ridiculously jealous.*

Ethan blew out a sigh. "Tell me about it."

"Is that why you let her take Laney?"

"She's a good sitter. I hired her a few times before this crush thing started. I have enough of a reputation to live down without someone thinking I'd play around with a high-school kid."

Before they could say more, a voice called out. "Molly! Is that really you?"

Lindsey Slater came toward them. Molly tensed, afraid that the sound of her name ringing through the gym would cause a tidal wave of disapproving glances. Not everyone was as kind-hearted as the Christmas tree farmer.

"Lindsey, hi." She glanced around nervously, expecting the worst. Ethan's strong fingers massaged the back of her neck, a comforting reminder that he was there and ready to leave at a moment's notice. All the more reason to hang tough and get through this if she could. Having her here mattered to Ethan.

To her relief, the only faces looking in her direction were either smiling or mildly curious. No one stared with condemning disapproval. Not yet anyway.

"Ethan said you might come," Lindsey said. "I'm really glad. We could use another guard on our team."

"I haven't played ball in a long time, Lindsey. I'm here only as a spectator tonight."

"Then I hope you'll think about rejoining soon. We're raising money to build a school in Mexico, and I can't play anymore until after the baby comes."

Molly's gaze went immediately to Lindsey's tummy. Happiness for the other woman, accompanied by a twinge of envy, slid through her. "I didn't know you were having a baby."

Lindsey laughed and touched the small mound protruding from beneath the oversized T-shirt. "You'd know these things if you'd come around more often."

Molly fell silent, not knowing how to respond. Didn't Lindsey and the others understand why she had stayed away?

Ethan, bless him, felt her discomfiture and filled the gap. "She's here tonight to help us out in the stands. Tom's team has all the noisy fans."

Lindsey laughed, and the awkward moment passed. "Most of that racket comes from his kids."

"Must be why Tom calls his team the Wild Bunch," Ethan joked.

Tom Castor was a popular local fireman with a competitive nature and a houseful of kids. He and his wife, Debbie, who waited tables at the diner, were mainstays of the church and worked tirelessly for the community. Molly had helped them with a number of charitable undertakings.

By this time several other people, including Pastor Cliff and his wife, Karen, had joined the conversation. No longer the focus of attention, Molly relaxed as the talk took hold and ebbed and flowed around her. It felt good to listen to small talk and the teasing banter of people who knew and trusted one another. She had missed this kind of thing more than she had realized.

From all appearances, Ethan was well liked and accepted. Not that Molly had doubted, but seeing him laugh and tease with other members of the church reaffirmed the kind of man she knew him to be. And the fact that he was cautiously kind to the gushing teenage Cass was, if she'd needed it, further proof of his integrity.

After a bit, Pastor Cliff clapped his hands once and rubbed his palms together in a gesture of anticipation. "You folks ready to get this show on the road?"

"Ready for the blood bath," Tom called, pumping one arm in the air to the groans and chuckles of those around him.

"In that case, tonight's devotional is all the more important," Cliff answered good-naturedly. "Gather round, everyone. I have a couple of verses from Romans and Second Corinthians. Then we'll pray and get the game started."

When the crowd of a hundred or more

people, both church regulars and community members who had come to support the good cause, had settled, Pastor Cliff read from the Bible and gave a brief talk about the relevance of the scripture to today's life.

Following prayer, he lifted a glowing face and a huge right arm and announced in oratorical style, "Let the games begin."

"Are you okay with this?" Ethan asked, before taking to the floor with his team. He stood a step below her, one sneakered foot raised to the bleacher. He looked awesome in loose sweat pants and a red basketball jersey emblazoned with the word Crossfire.

Trepidatious, but less anxious than before, Molly managed a smile. "I'll be fine."

He tilted his head toward the teenage Cass who sat a couple of rows behind Molly. "Will you keep an eye on Laney for me?"

Molly's confidence rose a couple of notches. She didn't understand why, but Ethan trusted her with his most prized possession. And she'd do anything to keep that trust.

"Should I go up and get her?"

"Nah. I don't want to hurt Cass's feelings. She or one of the other teenagers usually watch Laney while I play, but I feel better knowing you're here. Laney loves you." He squeezed her hand, and Molly thought he wanted to say more.

"I love her, too," she answered. It was true. She had fallen in love with the baby girl whose brown hair and blue eyes were so like her daddy's. She hadn't wanted ever to love another child the way she'd loved Zack, but she did. Surprisingly, the admission brought joy instead of pain. The risk of loving was a good thing.

"Wish me luck."

She lifted her hand for a high five. "You'll need it against Tom's team."

Ethan groaned. "*Et tu, Brute?*"

They both grinned as he jogged onto the gym floor.

"Mind if we sit here with you?" Lindsey asked as she and her little girl, Jade, slid onto the wooden bench next to Molly.

She'd always liked Lindsey, though the Christmas tree farmer was a little older, more Chloe's age than her own. They had been in the same singles' class until Jesse Slater came to town.

"I'd be glad for the company," Molly answered truthfully, relieved not to be left entirely alone.

"Ethan said you might."

"He talked to you about me?"

Lindsey shrugged. "Just said you were a little uncomfortable, having been away for so long."

Molly gazed out on the court at her delivery man, heart filling at his obvious thoughtfulness. So Ethan had paved the way to make this awkward evening easier for her.

"Ethan's a nice guy," she answered simply.

"I didn't know until last Sunday that you two were dating."

Molly sighed. She'd tried to convince herself that what she and Ethan were doing was not dating, but everyone else called it that. Might as well stop fooling herself.

"Oh, here they go." Lindsey sat forward in rapt attention as two men took center court for the tip-off. "Look, Jade. There's Daddy."

The game commenced in a crazy mix of camaraderie and competition. The Wild Bunch's fans did the wave and stomped the wooden bleachers hard enough to vibrate the entire gym. As Molly had expected, Ethan was a good athlete with a deadly three-point shot that kept Crossfire in the game.

At the half, with the Wild Bunch leading by five points, Ethan came up into the stands. Wiping his face with a towel, he plopped down beside Molly. Sweat plastered his shirt to his skin.

"You doin' okay?" he asked.

"Fine." And she was. Though several people had come by to talk, no one had mentioned Zack or Chloe. "Your team is hanging in there."

"Closest we've ever played the Wild Bunch. You must be our lucky charm." He tossed the towel over one shoulder. "Would you like a Coke or something?"

"You look like you could use one."

"You got that right." He hitched his chin toward the spot where Cass, flanked by two other girls, held Laney on her lap. "Let's grab the baby and head to the concession stand."

Molly followed him up the steps. Laney saw them coming and began to bounce and chatter, stretching tiny hands toward Molly. Her chest expanded with love for Ethan's child.

"Hey, wait a minute. What's with this?

You don't love Daddy anymore?" Ethan pretended hurt, but Molly could see he was pleased.

Snuggling the soft, warm body against her chest, Molly had to admit she was pleased, too. Carrying Laney, they headed to the lobby area.

Molly's plan to remain quiet and inconspicuous went out the window as they stopped over and over again to chat and laugh and joke about the crazy, unorthodox game. Ethan and his child were people magnets, and the community drew her back into the fold as if she'd never left.

Slowly, the awful weight of worry lifted from her shoulders. She had assumed the church sided with Chloe and hated her, but no one here was judging or condemning her. Here, at least, she could experience the warmth and joy of being part of a family, even if it wasn't the one she hungered for.

The spring evening was dark and cool by the time the game ended and they made their way to Molly's place. Ethan's heart was full. Tonight had done some good, he was sure of it. After the initial ice had been broken, Molly had seemed to enjoy herself, and he'd not only been glad, he'd been proud. In the good-natured atmosphere of a ball game, she'd gone from tense and anxious to heartrendingly grateful for the warm acceptance of the church members. It wasn't the same as reconciliation with her sister, but the plan he'd formulated with James was off to a good start. One step at a time, he would gradually push Molly forward.

In the glow of the dash lights, he admired the side of her face as she leaned over the seat to appease a tired and cranky Laney. The curve of her swingy hair brushed her chin and danced around her pretty mouth.

He thought of the last time he'd kissed her, that day when he'd told her about Twila. He'd known then that Molly was important to him and to Laney.

He wasn't much. Probably had no business getting involved with a decent girl like her, but his heart told him this was right.

He turned into the gravel drive and pulled to a stop in front of her house. The porch light glowed yellow as it had that first night months ago when he'd stumbled into her house out of the freezing cold.

He hadn't realized then, but he did now.

He'd been out in the cold emotionally at the time. He'd stopped trusting women, afraid they were all like Twila. But time with Molly, seeing her care for others, including him, had warmed his frozen, aching heart. Oh, she hadn't said she cared, but he was certain she did. He could feel it in everything she did. Even tonight, moving outside her comfort zone because he'd asked had proved that she cared.

Killing the motor, he turned in the seat. "I had a great time." He made a silly face. "Even if we did lose again."

She smiled. "Want to come inside for a while? Some hot chocolate might soothe your wounded pride."

"Better not." He hitched his chin toward the back seat. "The boss needs to hit the sack."

Molly laid a hand on his jacketed arm. Filled with an emotion too wonderful for words, she said, "Thank you for this, Ethan. As scared as I was to go to that game, I'm glad you talked me into it. For the first time in two years, I don't feel like people are saying bad things about me."

She realized now that the whispers and exclusion had mostly been in her mind, a part of her own guilt and self-punishment. She just hadn't been able to recognize the truth until now. If only the rift with Chloe was imaginary, everything would be great. But it wasn't. Tonight had helped, but her sister still hated her.

As if he read her thoughts, Ethan pulled her into his arms and said, "The situation with Chloe will improve. We have to keep praying, keep believing and keep being brave."

"I'm not all that brave."

"Sure you are. You were dynamite tonight. I was so proud of you."

"Really? I was proud of you, too." She'd felt more than pride. She'd felt special when his eyes had found hers during the game and they'd exchange smiles or she'd lift Laney's hand in a wave.

"See? We're great together. A regular team. You and me and Laney."

A team. She liked the sound of that.

"Molly," he started, then tipped his head back and stared at the truck's dark ceiling.

She touched his cheek, drew his face back down so that their eyes met in the faint light. "What?"

He smoothed her hair back, then bracketed

her face with both hands. The look in his eyes sent adrenaline swirling into her bloodstream.

"Maybe it's too soon to say this. Maybe I should never say this at all, considering my checkered past." He closed in so that his face was inches from hers. When he spoke, the words were but a breath of warmth against her lips. "I love you, Molly."

Her heart lurched, banging against her rib cage.

"Oh, Ethan." She touched his beloved cheek with the tips of her fingers.

In the next heartbeat, his mouth closed over hers in a kiss so full of sweet emotion that Molly wanted to cry. She loved him, too. Had loved him for a long time.

He was good for her in so many ways. Too good perhaps. And she wanted desperately to make him happy, to make up for the wrong Twila had done to him and Laney.

Laney.

The thought of the child stopped her cold.

How could Ethan even consider falling in love with someone like her? Wouldn't he always wonder in the back of his mind if Laney was safe? Wouldn't she?

When the kiss ended, his forehead tilted

against hers. “I know I’m no prize, and I have baggage that some women wouldn’t want to deal with—”

“Laney’s not baggage. She’s a treasure.” The very reason why his declaration scared her so much.

He kissed the tip of her nose. “She’s *my* treasure. I want her to be yours, too.”

She already was, but for Laney’s sake, Molly couldn’t say so. All the “what ifs” had begun to roll around inside her head again. What if she had a panic attack? What if something happened to Laney while she was in Molly’s care? Would Ethan still love her then?

Her hesitation wasn’t lost on Ethan. He backed off a little and asked, “Are you afraid you can’t love another woman’s child? Is that what’s bothering you?”

“No. Ethan, don’t think that. Don’t ever think that. I love that baby with all my heart.” Almost as if she was the woman who had given birth to Laney.

“Then what is it? Is it me? Is it because of the things I did before?”

“None of that. You’re a wonderful man. The problem isn’t you. It’s me.” She swallowed the lump in her throat and admitted, “I’m afraid of failing you.”

He gripped both of her hands in his. "Are you still worried that something will happen to Laney, and it will be your fault? Is that what this is all about?"

"Yes," she whispered, head down, embarrassed but relieved as well to admit the fear.

"Molly, sweetheart, no one can predict the future. But one thing I know. You would protect my baby girl with your life." He tapped her chin with a knuckle, lifting it. "Wouldn't you?"

"If I could."

"Then forget about everything else for a minute and answer me this. Do you care for me? I think you do, but I need you to say it."

"You know I do," she whispered. "Very much."

"Ah, Molly. You make me so happy." He kissed her again and, for a moment, her worries melted away in the warmth of his embrace.

"Remember the scripture Pastor Cliff read tonight?" he asked, eyes shining in the darkness.

Of course she remembered. She'd felt as though Cliff had picked that verse especially for her. "There is now no condemnation to those who are in Christ Jesus…Old things are passed away and all things are new."

Happiness bloomed inside Molly. Ethan was right. She couldn't go back, but she could move forward. She'd taken the first step by renewing her church friendships, and, as a result some of her pain and guilt had disappeared. Best of all, she hadn't had a panic attack in months, a sign that they were gone for good.

Overjoyed and filled with love for this man who'd given her hope, she threw herself into his arms. When he laughed with joy, she laughed with him.

Maybe, just maybe, they could make this work.

Chapter Twelve

Rain threatened all night before the Easter sunrise service. About an hour before dawn, to the relief of several hundred people, the clouds cleared.

As they had each year for longer than anyone could remember, every church in town had come together in a cooperative effort to present the pageant. Ethan and all the other actors and musicians had practiced for weeks. The play, which had begun last night with the story of the crucifixion, would conclude this morning with the resurrection. Cars, people, lawn chairs and blankets speckled the darkened hillside outside Winding Stair where the dramatic retelling would occur.

Since the basketball game and Ethan's beautiful declaration of love, they had attended two church services together. Today was the third. Returning to her family's church was the scariest, most wonderful thing she'd done in ages, but if she and Ethan were to have any hope of a future together, getting her spiritual life on track had to come first.

When she had fretted about her sister's possible reaction to her return, Ethan, bless him, had talked to James on the telephone. Chloe had been told and the choice to attend church or not would be hers.

Sadly, her sister had chosen to stay away. The idea hurt, as Chloe's rejection always did, but Molly stiffened her resolve and attended anyway. She loved her sister and would try until her dying day to reconcile, but she refused to be a party to Chloe's bitterness any longer.

Molly scanned this morning's crowd for a glimpse of her sister or mother and came up empty. The gathering was large enough to hide in, though, so perhaps Chloe had ventured out. Molly hoped so. The beauty of a sunrise service was good for the soul.

"Your baby is darling," a woman murmured as Molly opened her lawn chair and settled into it with Laney on her lap.

"She's not my—" She started to explain and then changed her mind. Why bother? Laney belonged to her heart and that was what counted. "Thank you," she said instead.

Aunt Patsy, who had ridden to the service with Molly and Ethan, set her lawn chair on the opposite side. Holding on to the plastic arms for support, she eased down. Molly knew her great-aunt's knees bothered her something fierce, but she would never complain.

She leaned toward Molly and whispered, "Laney looks precious in that outfit you bought."

Molly had spent hours on the Internet searching for the perfect Easter dress for Ethan's baby. She'd finally found the pink-and-white confection complete with lacy bonnet, white tights and patent-leather shoes. The price had been shocking, but Ethan's reaction had been worth the cost and effort. He'd thanked her with so many kisses, she'd blushed.

A disembodied voice, sounding much like Pastor Cliff's, opened the service, and a holy hush settled over the crowd. In the gray dawn, Molly watched with rapt attention as a hill outside of Winding Stair, Oklahoma, was transformed into ancient Jerusalem. Against the lighted backdrop of three wooden crosses and a cave-like tomb, ministers gave readings, and a chorus of voices swelled in song.

At exactly the right moment, when the mother of Jesus approached the tomb weeping, sunlight broke over the horizon in beams so radiant that some folks later said that God Himself smiled on the day. The stone rolled away from the tomb and the choir began to sing "He Is Risen" with such power and passion that goose bumps prickled Molly's arms.

She pondered the symbolism of Jesus as the sacrificial Lamb who came that mankind might be reunited with a Holy God, of the new beginnings made possible by His life and death and resurrection, of all the fresh possibilities embodied in Easter.

She thought of her own new beginnings, too, and a wonderful peace enfolded her. As the light of the new day spread across the land and the service concluded in glorious song, Molly felt as though she, too, had come out of a dark place and into a marvelous light.

She hugged Laney to her chest and closed her eyes in gratitude.

As the quiet crowd slowly broke up, going separate ways to contemplate the holiness of Easter Sunday, Ethan, in his long governor's robes, joined her.

He hunkered down in front of her chair and took Laney into his arms. The baby's ruffles and lace made crinkling noises as he rubbed his nose against her neck.

"What did you think? Did it look all right from out here?" The eagerness in him was boyish and charming.

"Ethan, it was awesome. You were awesome. I've never been to such a beautiful pageant."

"Neither have I," he said, grinning. "But then, this is my first and only Easter pageant."

Aunt Patsy reached over and patted his arm. "Well, it won't be your last. You made a formidable Pontius Pilate."

"Why, thank you, Miss Patsy." He bowed his head in mock humility. Laney grabbed one ear and twisted. With a yelp, Ethan unwound the tiny fingers. "Are you girls as hungry as I am?"

Molly rose and folded her lawn chair, then took Laney from Ethan while he assisted Aunt Patsy. "Probably not, but coffee sounds good."

"The church has coffee and rolls waiting. That should hold us until ten."

Although they were not technically a couple, they had promised Lindsey and Jesse to eat brunch with the young couples' class at ten. Later in the afternoon, the church was hosting a giant Easter-egg hunt for all the kids. Aunt Patsy and her group of friends had spent hours stuffing plastic eggs for the event.

"It's going to be a busy day."

"But a good one."

"We've got to get some pictures of that baby in her finery," Aunt Patsy said as they walked toward the parking area. "She'll only have one first Easter."

Ethan stopped in his tracks and turned to face the hillside, now washed in bright sunlight. "I just thought of something. This is my first Easter, too. The first one that ever meant anything."

Molly understood his awe. Even though she had been a Christian for a long time, today felt like a renewal to her, too.

Smiling up at him, she hooked her arm through his. “Pretty cool, huh?”

“Yeah.” His gaze shifted to Laney, lying across Molly’s shoulder. “You want me to carry her?”

“No. We’re fine.” And they were, just as they had been for sometime now. She could hold Laney and love her without a racing pulse or the awful tightness in her chest and throat. She’d almost stopped worrying that something terrible would happen.

She hugged the bundle of ruffles and lace a little closer.

When they reached the parking area other members of the cast milled about. The rise and fall of voices mingled with engines cranking and doors slamming. A man in Roman centurion gear called out and Ethan drifted off to speak with him.

Molly unlocked the car and bent to fasten Laney in her car seat. When she straightened, Aunt Patsy stood on the opposite side of the vehicle in conversation with an older woman Molly recognized from their church.

“I don’t really think that’s any of your concern, Hazel,” she heard Aunt Patsy say.

“It’s not right, I tell you, Patsy. That boy

has his nerve dating a decent girl like Molly. He never did marry that baby's mother, you know." She announced the fact in a low, gossipy tone as if she hoped it was news to her listener.

"I know." Aunt Patsy's rosy cheeks grew redder, a sign, Molly knew, that she was getting angry. "I know about a lot of other things, too, that you apparently have forgotten. Things like Christian charity and forgiveness."

"Oh forevermore, Patsy." Hazel drew herself up in a straight line. "I would think as her aunt, you would be more concerned about that niece of yours. She's had enough trouble without getting involved with a philanderer who goes around making illegitimate babies."

"It's Easter, Hazel. I suggest you think about what that means and let the Lord worry about Ethan and Molly." Aunt Patsy turned her back on the woman, opened the car door and got in, slamming it a little harder than necessary.

As Hazel stalked away, gait stiff and insulted, Molly noticed what she'd missed during the confrontation. Ethan. Standing at the back of the car, expression stricken.

Molly's stomach hurt and her knees trembled for him. She was angry at the woman but ached for Ethan.

"I'm so sorry," she said, going to him. "She shouldn't have said that."

His jaw flexed. "I'm okay. I've heard worse."

He had? "What she said was cruel and wrong. She hurt your feelings."

He jerked one shoulder. "I have thick skin."

Not all that thick. She could see he was disturbed. Words wounded, even when they were untrue and the recipient didn't deserve them.

"Come on," Ethan said with false joviality, tugging on her hand. "I'm starving."

Molly tiptoed up on her new spring shoes to kiss his cheek.

"I love you," she whispered against his freshly shaved skin. No matter what anyone else thought of him or of his former life, Ethan Hunter was a good man.

Ethan rubbed his cheek, his eyebrows arching high. Mischief replaced the hurt in his eyes. "Maybe being gossiped about is not so bad after all."

"And then again, maybe it is. But there isn't a thing you can do about it anyway."

"Except to win her over with my devastating charm."

Gesturing to his robes, Molly teased, "You're Pontius Pilate. You could have her executed."

"No," he said. "Banished. No Easter-egg hunt for her. No chocolate bunnies. No marshmallow eggs."

Molly pressed a hand to her heart in pretend horror. "Cruel and unusual punishment. You are a wicked ruler indeed."

They both laughed and climbed inside the car, letting the banter soften the sting of the woman's cruel comments. At least for now.

By six o'clock that evening, Molly had eaten more chocolate bunnies and marshmallow eggs than she could count. She had also, along with Ethan, participated in an adult egg hunt at the Slater Farm that had been more fun than she thought possible. Who would believe grown men would tackle one another in pursuit of a plastic, candy-filled egg?

Now, as she plopped down on the couch in Ethan's apartment and kicked off her shoes, she said, "Wasn't this a great day?"

She leaned back and ran both hands through her messy hair, tired but content.

Ethan stood in the adjoining kitchenette, staring into the refrigerator. When he looked up and smiled, Molly's heart did a happy dance.

"Aren't you glad you went?"

"Mmm. Very glad. What are you doing in there?"

"Making the queen a bottle. She'll wake up howling any minute."

"After the day she's had, being passed from person to person and played with by every kid in town, I thought she might sleep all night."

"She will after she eats." He added cereal to the bottle and gave it a shake. "There she goes."

Sure enough, a restless whimper turned to a loud howl. Ethan plunked the bottle onto the coffee table, trotted to the small nursery and returned with a squirming, squawling baby.

"Let me have her," Molly said, holding up her arms. "I'll feed her."

Something she'd never thought possible had happened. She wanted to hold and feed a baby. For once, the fear only flitted across her mind and disappeared.

Ethan's smile lit the living room. He tossed the burp towel over her shoulder, lowered Laney into her arms, and handed her the bottle. The baby's pudgy hands batted at her dinner, trying to pull it into her mouth.

"Hold on, Miss Greedy." Molly slid the nipple between the bow lips.

"There you go," she crooned. "There you go."

Ethan stood before them, smiling down. "You two look all cozy."

"We are." She kissed Laney's forehead. "Aren't we, sweetie pie?"

Laney's answer came in contented slurps and grunts.

"I'm gonna run out to the truck for a minute," Ethan said. "To get that CD Jesse loaned me. Be right back, okay?"

Molly tensed. It had been a while since she'd been alone with Laney, but she loved Ethan and if they were to have any future together, she had to take care of his baby—alone. The attacks were gone. She needed to act as though they were.

"Sure. Go ahead. I wanted to listen to it, too."

He bent forward to kiss her hair. The pleasant mingle of aftershave and chocolatey marshmallow made her smile.

As he slipped out into the darkness, Molly rocked back and forth and hummed a lullaby. Laney's blue eyes stared wide and intent.

Without warning, the tiny face mottled. Laney coughed, sputtering cereal-laced formula onto Molly's hands.

Molly jerked the bottle from the baby's mouth and sat her upright, patting her back. Laney coughed and struggled, pushing air out but never inhaling.

Molly's pulse clattered into her throat. Laney was choking. Strangling.

"Ethan," she screamed. "Ethan, help!"

She flipped the baby over and dangled her across her knees. With the heel of one hand, she applied a not-so-gentle rap to the center of Laney's back.

Laney coughed again and then began to cry. Loud, wailing cries rent the apartment.

Ethan's footsteps thundered from outside. The door slammed open on its hinges. "What's wrong? What happened?"

He rushed to her side, jerking Laney upright.

"She choked. She choked." Molly's voice shook with fear.

Ethan made a quick examination of the baby. "She's okay now."

But Molly wasn't.

What if she hadn't been able to stop the choking? What if Laney had died? What if…

Her chest tightened and her hands began to tremble.

Oh, no. Oh, no, no, no. Not the panic. Not now. Not in front of Ethan.

The tingling crept into her fingers like millions of crawling ants. Fear, terrible and consuming, gripped her.

"Molly?" He frowned, concerned. "Laney's okay. Calm down."

She shook her head at him, humiliated, terrified. It was happening and Ethan would see. He would know her shame, her weakness.

She jumped up and rushed out of the room. She'd no more than reached the back bedroom when a tidal wave of panic closed in. Her heart thundered faster and faster. Sweat beaded her face, her hands and knees trembled as violently as an earthquake. Her throat closed tighter and tighter.

What if another baby had died in her care?

She stumbled toward the wall. Spots danced in front of her eyes.

"Molly?" Ethan came through the door, and she longed for the floor to open and swallow her up. He reached for her, his face full of concern. "What's wrong?"

She pushed him away. He was blocking the air, crowding her. "I can't breathe. I can't breathe."

She was going to die this time. She wanted to.

He grabbed her shoulders, squared her toward him. She fought at his hands. They smothered her, cut off her oxygen.

"Talk to me. What's happening?"

"I can't breathe. Go away. Take care of Laney."

"Laney is fine, I tell you. She's fine. Now calm down."

She fought away from him, turned her back and went to her knees, shaking too hard to stand. But lying down strangled her. She had to prop up, get air. Her heart hammered incessantly, wildly. She was smothering. Dying.

Suddenly, strong hands lifted her up and whirled her around, bracing her back against the wall. Ethan dropped to the floor beside her.

He grasped her chin in his hard fingers,

forced her face up. "Has this happened before?"

She nodded. "Can't breathe."

"Panic attack," he said, making a paramedic's quick assessment. "Listen to me. Let me help."

She nodded again. What else could she do? He was here. He'd witnessed her shame.

"You're hyperventilating. Breathe into this bag." From somewhere he produced a paper bag and cupped it around her mouth.

"Take a long, deep belly breath," he said, laying a hand over her abdomen.

Molly shook her head frantically, wanting to scream. How could she take a deep breath? She was strangling.

"Do it," he commanded in a voice that brooked no argument. "Look into my eyes and take one long deep breath. Now."

She locked eyes with him and did as he commanded. It wasn't easy, but she did it.

"Good girl. Do it again. Only this time, in your mind, count backwards starting at twenty. With every number think of someone you care about. Concentrate on that. Visualize that."

Twenty. She thought of Ethan.

Nineteen. Laney.

Oh, dear Lord, what if Laney had choked to death?

Her fingers tightened on the paper bag. She started to pant again.

Ethan tapped her knuckles. "Relax, Molly. Don't pant. Breathe, slow and easy. This is going to pass. You will get through this and be all right."

She nodded again, concentrated on the soothing encouragement in his voice.

"Count for me. What are you on?"

"Eighteen." *Aunt Patsy.*

"Good. Keep counting. Concentrate on good things, good places, good people. Count your blessings."

Seventeen. The smiles of children when they opened the boxes she sent.

Sixteen. The seniors who made her laugh and told her stories.

"You're doing fine, sweetheart. It's passing." Ethan stroked her shoulders in circular movements, soothing, calming. She took another deep, cleansing breath.

Thirteen. Daddy. Oh, how she missed that laugh.

By the time she'd counted backward to nine the tightness in her chest began to subside. Knees up, she dropped her head back against the cool plaster. There was a water spot on the ceiling of his apartment. She studied it, concentrated on it. Did Ethan know his roof had leaked at some point? Maybe during the ice storm?

Ethan's voice rumbled on, a low purr in her ear.

At three, the fear dissipated. Her pulse slowed. She laid the paper sack aside.

"You're not trembling anymore."

"I'm better now." She couldn't meet his eyes.

In the other room, Laney began to cry.

"Go." Molly pushed at him. "Take care of her. Hurry."

Ethan studied her face as if weighing which hysterical female needed him the most. "Stay put."

He left the room and Molly wished she had the strength to get up and leave. Before she could even try, Laney quieted and Ethan returned.

He hunkered down beside her. "How long has this been going on?"

Her chest started to hurt again. "Is Laney okay?"

"She's fine." His sweet face was stern. "Answer my question. How long?"

"Since Zack died. I thought I was well. I thought they were gone."

But they weren't. A few minutes alone with Laney had brought them back in full force. She would always be in danger around babies. She'd accepted that before Ethan came along. And now look what had happened the minute she'd let her guard down.

"Have you seen a doctor about it?"

She nodded, picking at a stray carpet thread. "Yes, but I don't like pills."

"What about therapy?"

"That, too. For a while."

The only thing that ever really helped was staying away from her sister and children, the triggers as her therapist called them. As long as she was at home on the farm or working in the center, she was fine. Every book she'd read and every doctor she'd seen had insisted avoidance was not the answer. But they were wrong. Hadn't this incident proved as much?

She pushed up off the floor and went into the kitchen for a drink of water. Her legs felt like cooked noodles.

Ethan followed, attentive and watchful. She appreciated his concern, but the sooner she got away from him the better off they'd both be.

Gripping the counter with one hand, she tipped her head back and let the cool water wash away any residual tightness in her throat. Too bad it couldn't wash away the attacks, but she was trapped in a vicious prison of fear that nothing could eliminate. Nothing except avoidance.

She drained the glass then set it in the sink. With the clink of glass against porcelain, she stared at the white tile backsplash and said, "I need to go home."

"Are you sure you're ready to be alone?"

"I have to get away from here, Ethan." She managed a glance at him. Then wished she hadn't.

He studied her, worried, uncertain and loving. Right now, she didn't want him to love her. She wanted him to let her go.

"Okay," he said, slowly, as if trying to gauge her mood. "If you want to go home, I'll drive you."

"No need," she said, a little too sharply, but why prolong the agony. "I can drive myself."

She'd driven her Jeep into town because it had more room than Ethan's truck, and now she was glad she had. Making her escape back to safety would be easier.

Gently, Ethan gripped her arms and turned her to face him. "I won't take no for an answer, Molly. I want to help. You're upset. I don't want you to be alone."

"I said I can drive myself, Ethan. I don't need you."

What a terrible lie that was, but it stopped him cold. He dropped his arms and stood inches away, his wounded expression a jab at her already tattered heart. He looked so confused, and she hated herself for letting their relationship come this far.

For a short, beautiful time she'd believed they could make it. She loved him. Never wanted to see him hurt.

All the more reason to get this over with. Tonight had proven that a relationship between her and a man with a child would never work.

The sooner she got away from Ethan and Laney, the better for them all. She'd thought she was well. She'd thought her love for Ethan and Laney made all the difference. But love wasn't enough to heal what was wrong with her.

Gathering her purse, she started to the

door. Ethan followed, worried. “I wish you’d stay a little longer or let me go with you. You’re still pale as a ghost.”

“I’m fine. Take care of your baby.”

“Call me when you get home.”

She shook her head. “I don’t think so.”

He reached for her, but she backed away. A tide of emotion already threatened to destroy her resolve. If he touched her, she’d fall apart.

“Goodbye, Ethan. I’m sorry.”

Before he could stop her, she fumbled the door open and rushed out into the parking lot to her Jeep.

Hands shaking, she started the vehicle and shifted into gear.

It was over. She couldn’t take any more chances. The brief and lovely dream with Ethan was over for good. Eyes dry and hot with unshed tears, she headed out of the parking lot and into the gaping emptiness of her future.

Chapter Thirteen

Ethan spent the next hour pacing the floor, praying, thinking and trying to understand what had happened with Molly.

Their day had been amazing. With every minute together, he fell more in love with her. She was silly and warm and kind. And she loved him. He was certain of that.

But something far more serious than a panic attack had occurred tonight. Something had happened inside that pretty head of hers that she wasn't sharing with him. Her goodbye sounded too permanent.

A sick churning started in the pit of his stomach.

He paced into the tiny nursery and gazed down at Laney, his heart filling with wonder at this gift from God. The spill of light from the hallway washed over her face, and her long eyelashes cast shadows on her cheekbones. She slept in that relaxed way of babies, knees tucked to her chest, bottom in the air.

Molly said she had choked, but by the time he'd come in, she was fine. Except for the formula and cereal on her face and bib, he couldn't tell anything unusual had occurred.

But whatever had happened had been enough to send Molly into a state of panic. The aftermath of cold aloofness had been every bit as scary to him as the panic attack.

A colorful mobile, a gift from Molly, circled over the crib. The music box of lullabies had long since wound down. Absently, he tapped a dangling monkey with one finger.

Molly's behavior disturbed him. Why hadn't she let him drive her home? Why had she left so abruptly?

Was she giving up on them?

Spinning around, he went to the living room and picked up the phone. He would never sleep until he knew she was all right anyway. Might as well get some answers.

She picked up on the second ring. Some of the tension left his shoulders.

"Molly. It's me. Ethan."

"I know."

"Are you all right?"

"Yes." Her answer was curt as though she didn't want to talk. He wasn't having that.

"Talk to me."

"I'm really tired."

"Me, too. It was a great day, huh?"

He tried to sound upbeat and casual. Maybe if he could get her talking about the day everything would normalize. "How about coming over tomorrow night? We'll rent a video."

"Ethan." Her voice sounded distant. "I'm not coming over anymore."

She was starting to scare him. "Because of a little anxiety attack?"

"I thought Laney was going to die. I thought I was going to cause another child's death."

His stomach started churning again.

"You were not responsible for her choking, Molly, any more than you were responsible for Zack's death. Don't you see that? Laney's choked on me before. And yeah, I'll admit, it's scary, but she gets over it." He walked to the window and pushed the drapes aside. "You have to do the same."

"I can't."

"Can't? Or won't?"

"If something happened to her in my care, I would lose my mind, Ethan. I can't live through that again." The tiny quiver in her voice got to him in a hurry. "Please. Just let me go."

His grip tightened on the receiver. She was upset and as a result, unreasonable. Surely, she wasn't saying what he thought she was.

"What do you mean, let you go? We can work this out."

"We can't. I can't. Don't you understand? You have a child. I can never be alone with a baby again. Ever."

He'd thought Molly was different, but like Twila she didn't want his child.

He shoved the drapes farther apart and pressed his forehead against the cool glass windowpane. A sense of doom as dark as the street outside descended.

"Laney and I are a package deal. You knew that from the start."

"Yes, I did. And that's the way it should be. I'm sorry."

"But you love me." He ground his teeth in frustration.

She loved him but not his kid. He'd heard that before.

"I do love you. And I love Laney." She sucked in a deep breath, and he braced himself knowing instinctively that the worst was yet to come. "That's why we have to end this now before it's too late."

She loved him. She loved Laney. But she was willing to give them both up. And why? Because of fear? Because she was afraid Laney would die in her care?

He slammed a fist against the window facing. "This is crazy, Molly. It makes no sense."

"It does to me."

"Don't make a decision tonight while you're upset. Take some time. Pray about it."

"I already have. And look what happened."

She was starting to tick him off. "God didn't cause that baby to choke, and He doesn't cause your panic attacks."

"Do you think you have the answer to everything? If God cared—" She stopped, ending with a sob.

Ethan reined in his emotions. Going off half-cocked could only cause more trouble. He had the scars to prove it.

With intentional gentleness, he said, "Blaming God won't solve anything."

"I'm not blaming God."

"Aren't you?"

"I don't know what you mean. You're the one not making sense now."

"You think God has let you down, first when Zack died and then when your family turned against you. Now you think he's done it again. But He didn't. He sent Laney and me along to make things better, not worse. You have to trust that everything will work out for the best."

Ethan wasn't sure where the ideas came from, but he knew he had hit the nail on the head. Somewhere in all the tragedy Molly had lost her trust in God's ultimate goodness.

Her end of the phone hummed with silence. Finally, she whispered, "I don't know what to believe anymore."

"Then let me tell you. Believe that I love you. Believe that God loves you. And together the three of us can work through any problems we encounter. Nothing's too big for God. I'm living proof of that."

"I can't take the chance again, Ethan." Her voice was small and lonely. "Look what happened."

"Avoiding the problem is not rational. And it won't fix things."

"It's the only way I know how to cope."

He was starting to get desperate here. Really desperate.

"That's not coping. That's hiding. Existing in a tiny realm of perceived safety, terrified of seeing a baby or your sister or anything that might trigger an attack."

He couldn't believe this was happening. Not again. Another woman tossing him aside like yesterday's hamburger wrapper. Only this time he loved that woman and she loved him. And she loved Laney, too, so much that she feared harming her.

His palms grew damp against the telephone. "Don't do this, Molly." He wasn't too proud to beg. "Don't throw away something beautiful and right."

"It's over, Ethan. I'm sorry." Sobs broke free. "So sorry."

And the line went dead in his ear.

Ethan sat in the darkened living room for hours staring at the wall and watching the occasional sweep of car lights beam in from the parking lot. The refrigerator kicked on. The ice maker dumped. Once, Laney whimpered in her sleep.

He wanted to do the same. Whimper like a kicked dog, then go to sleep and pray that tonight was all a bad dream.

No matter how he examined the situation with Molly, he came away without an answer. He rubbed a hand over his chest. It hurt.

After the ordeal with Twila he'd vowed to be smarter about women.

He gave a huff of self-reproach. There was his answer plain as day.

As cruel as she'd been, the woman in the parking lot after the sunrise service had been right. A man with his tainted past had no business falling in love with a nice girl like Molly.

If he'd listened to his common sense, none of this would have happened.

He drew in a deep breath and let it out slowly. All the common sense in the world wouldn't change one thing. He loved Molly. Being with her energized him and gave him hope for a better future. She was the other half of his heart. Giving her up without a fight was out of the question.

But was it unfair to pursue her? Was God trying to tell him that he was wrong for Molly?

Taking his Bible, he flipped it open, thumbed through the pages looking for comfort or guidance. Nothing caught his eye. He closed it again, laced his fingers and leaned forward, head down, hands dangling between his knees.

"I am one messed-up dude, Lord," he said. "I sure could use some help."

Inexplicably, the words *Joy comes in the morning,* filtered through his head. He frowned in thought. Was that in the Bible? Had he heard it somewhere?

He didn't know about joy, but for certain daylight would come in the morning and with it a ten-hour day of driving.

He stood and stretched his back.

"Just me and You, Lord," he murmured. "Just me and You all over again." And then because he could do nothing else, he went to bed.

Morning came and went, but Ethan didn't feel a bit of joy. He'd awakened with a headache and a knot in his belly that he hadn't been able to shake. When his lunch went sour on him, he'd pulled into a quick-stop for antacids and chewed a handful of the chalky tablets, washing them down with bottled water.

Molly was on his mind all day, and he'd vacillated between anger, pity and prayer.

He drove by her workplace, saw her Jeep in the lot, and thought of going inside. He could confront her, make her listen to reason. He loved her. He could make her happy.

But the voice in his head stopped him. Maybe he couldn't make any woman happy. Hadn't he failed miserably with Twila?

By late afternoon, he wheeled his van down the streets of Winding Stair ahead of schedule. He'd made good time today regardless of his heavy-hearted mood.

As if on automatic pilot, he turned down Cedar Street toward Miss Patsy's apartment. A check of his watch said he could stop for a minute. He wasn't sure what he would say.

She came to the door, wearing her rosy-cheeked smile and a jogging suit with dirty knees. In one hand she carried a large wooden bird house.

"Just the man I was wishing for," she said

as he slammed out of the truck and started up the incline.

His spirits lifted. Molly's aunt had that effect on just about everybody. "What are you up to, Miss Patsy?"

"Oh, I was out here puttering around in these flower beds when I saw those red wasps trying to take over my martin house. Thought I'd better clean it out. Now I can't get it back up on the post."

Ethan took the tiny apartment house from her. "How did you get it down?"

She waved him off. "Don't ask. Molly would wring my neck if she knew."

"I probably would too," he answered with a grin. A stepladder leaned against the side of the house, the obvious culprit. He took it and started up.

Patsy stood beneath him, head tilted back. "Yesterday was sure a wonderful Easter, wasn't it?"

With his shins balanced against the top of the ladder, Ethan set the birdhouse onto the pole and fastened it down.

How could he answer her question? Yesterday had been great. And it had been terrible.

He gave the pole a shake and, satisfied

that the house was stable, descended the ladder.

"Molly had a panic attack last night," he said without preliminaries.

The older lady's face twisted with dismay. "I guess she'd never told you about them?"

"No. I had known something was wrong as far back as the night of the ice storm, but she never said a word."

"She hasn't had one in a long time."

"That's what she told me." He rubbed the dust from his hands.

"Is she all right this morning?"

"I don't know."

"Why not? Didn't you give her a call?"

He looked up at the birdhouse, down at the greening grass, and then into Miss Patsy's wise eyes. Here was a mentor he'd always been able to talk to, even about her own niece.

"She broke things off. Said she couldn't take the chance."

Behind her wire-framed glasses, Patsy frowned. "Of what?"

He lifted the ladder and carried it to the front porch. Patsy walked alongside him.

"That's what I asked. And her answer was

all confused. She's afraid she'll hurt Laney. She's afraid the panic attacks will start again." He didn't understand well enough to explain.

"That's a bunch of nonsense."

He leaned the ladder against the alcove next to Miss Patsy's gardening tools, waiting for the metallic clatter to subside before he spoke again.

"I know it. You know it. But Molly doesn't."

"She's walked a hard, lonely road in the last two years, but since you came along she's been happier, better. Just look at how you've gotten her out of that house and back involved with the church and with people. Don't give up on her, Ethan. Give her a little more time."

Ethan wished it was that simple. Patience he could do. Time he could do. He leaned against the porch post, pondering the question that had haunted him all night. Even if those things would bring her around, did he have a right to be with her?

An old faded green metal chair sat at one end of the porch. With a scrape of metal against concrete, Patsy twisted it toward him and sat down.

"You love her, don't

"Yeah. I do." He ran

hair. He'd even been

marriage. Now there was

"And she loves you," P

matter-of-fact manner of

is, she's crazy about you a

can tell by the way she look

you aren't paying attention.

you going to do about it?"

He gnawed the inside of his

thought about the question. He knew what he wanted to do. He wanted to tell Molly that nothing she could do, short of denying she loved him, would drive him away. He could wait forever if he had to.

His answer wasn't as optimistic. "Nothing."

"Nothing? Boy, what are you talking about? You don't know how long I've been waiting and praying for the right man to come along and sweep that niece of mine off her feet."

"That's the problem, Miss Patsy. I'm not the right man for Molly."

"What makes you think such a silly thing?"

He hitched one shoulder. "Molly's a nice

her

her

earring
ghed and
ing on with
you, Ethan. ... is old woman
and you listen good.

White tennis shoes squared, she leaned forward and pointed out at the brown van.

"See those mirrors on your truck? God doesn't have those. Some people do, but God don't. He never looks back at what you've done, only forward to the good you're doing now. There's no Reverse in God's kingdom."

Ethan allowed a smile. Miss Patsy had a way of laying out the gospel unlike any he'd ever heard.

"Are you saying that God doesn't hold my mistake against me? That He isn't trying to tell me I'm not good enough for Molly?"

Dear Reader,

I hope you enjoyed the second story of my Sisters Of The Heart series. In the first book of the series, *His Saving Grace,* Gracie finally woke up Jack, the man she'd loved for years, and, finally, he had enough sense to claim her as his own. At their wedding in the end of *Testing His Patience,* I introduced Connie, the third "sister of the heart." The final book will be her story. Look for *Loving Constance* in November 2004.

Gil and Patience carried a lot of "baggage." But the largest was a lack of forgiveness. It's hardest to forgive those who hurt us the most. However, we know we must forgive because Christ loved us first and forgave us. Forgiving isn't easy unless we remember that forgiving someone who has hurt us really frees us—once and for all—from the power of past pain. It brings hope and new life.

Forgiveness isn't saying wrong wasn't done; it's just letting go of our anger, cleaning it out of our lives and our souls. Let God take care of the reckoning, as in the Lord's Prayer—"Forgive us our trespasses as we forgive those who trespass against us." A tall order, but a necessary one.

Blessings,

Lyn Cote

"That's exactly what I'm saying. Oh, some people will criticize no matter what you do, but you have to give it to God. Move on. Put the past to rest once and for all."

"But part of my past will always be with me."

"The Lord has a purpose in all things, even mistakes or tragedies. Now, I'm not saying He causes them, but I do know that He takes anything that happens in our lives and works something good from it. Just look at you and Laney. Isn't she worth the trouble? Aren't you glad she's in your life, no matter how she got there?"

The light inside Ethan came on as bright as if the sun rose in his chest. When he'd turned his life over to the Lord, the nightmare with Twila had culminated in a beautiful thing—his daughter. Then, from the ashes of his unrestrained lifestyle, a new and better man had risen.

"I've been as bad as Molly about hanging on to guilt, haven't I?"

"Most likely. But if we trust Him, the Lord will take us from where we are to where He plans for us to be. And it's always better than anything we can imagine."

Patsy was right. Even the time in his life that began as a mistake had become his greatest blessing—Laney.

"I think Molly's struggling with that, too, Miss Patsy. Because of all that's happened she's lost confidence that God has her best interest at heart."

Hadn't he almost done the same?

"Well, mark my words. The Lord has a plan. You and me have just got to be smart enough not to get in His way."

"I can't make her want me and Laney."

"No, you can't." She pushed up out of the chair and came to him. "But I'm asking you as a friend, Ethan. Don't give up yet. Give her some space and some time. And keep on praying."

"What if she never comes around?"

"What if she does?"

He laughed, surprised at the simple logic. "How did you get so smart?"

She patted his arm. "Life's a good teacher. I've learned a few things through my own blunders."

"Not you," he said, gently teasing.

She swatted his arm. "Get going, you big lug. People want their stuff delivered on time."

He pulled her to him for a quick kiss on the cheek. "Thanks, Miss Patsy."

Face flushed with pleasure, she flapped her hands. "Go on now. And bring that baby by sometime soon."

Ethan executed a smart salute. "Yes, ma'am."

As he jogged to his truck, Miss Patsy's cleansing words circled inside his head and took root. God never looks back. And he shouldn't either. He was doing his best to walk in God's will, and he had to believe Molly was a part of that.

Time would tell if Molly could overcome her fears, and learn to trust.

And if there was one thing Ethan had, it was time.

Chapter Fourteen

Molly spotted Ethan and Laney the moment she arrived at the church picnic. Her traitorous heart leaped to see how handsome Ethan looked in a plaid shirt hanging open over a white T-shirt and a pair of ordinary jeans. His wide white smile flashed at something Pastor Cliff said when he placed Laney in the outstretched arms of the pastor's wife.

Molly's arms ached to be the ones holding Laney. And she wanted to talk to Ethan so badly her throat hurt.

Not for the first time, she questioned the wisdom of attending this annual event. For a week after the break-up with Ethan she'd confined herself to home and work. Then

Aunt Patsy had gotten hold of her. This time she hadn't been gentle. Worse still, Aunt Patsy had cried, and Molly couldn't stand to see her beloved aunt upset. Not if she could do something to prevent it. So she'd gone back to church again.

Chloe hadn't been happy, but Molly had kept her distance and soldiered on. If she'd learned anything, it was that she needed her church family and she needed God. Ethan said she'd stopped trusting God, but he was wrong. She trusted God. It was herself she didn't trust.

Strangely, glimpsing Ethan across the churchyard or in the foyer had proven harder than dealing with Chloe's silent stares. Sometimes he said hello, his blue eyes full of hurt. Those days she'd go home and cry.

She'd known he would be here today and thought she was prepared to see him. Now she wasn't so sure she could get through an afternoon with Ethan so close—and yet so far away. Keeping her commitment to let him go was the hardest thing she'd done in a long time. And she had done some difficult things.

The day after Easter he'd sent flowers. Yellow tulips. She'd cried that day, too. His phone calls, every day for a while, had dwindled away to none at all now. Perhaps he'd given up on her. Maybe he'd even found someone else.

Molly ran nervous palms down the side of her jeans and considered getting back into the Jeep.

"Don't even think about it."

Molly swiveled around to find Lindsey Slater coming across the dirt road, her pregnancy noticeable beneath a big T-shirt advertising her Christmas-tree farm.

"Come on. We need some help getting all the food organized. Church folks do love to eat."

A horde of people surrounded the concrete tables beneath a huge pavilion complete with outdoor grill. Pastor Cliff manned the grill, his booming laugh as pleasant as the scent of burgers. Ice chests filled with pop and water would be put to good use throughout the afternoon.

Two men were setting up a volleyball net while some of the older folks pitched horseshoes and the kids chased each other in circles, yelling at the top of their lungs.

The lake, about a hundred yards away, was still too cold for swimming, but the late-spring day was warm and sunny enough for a potluck picnic.

"I brought cake," she said, reaching into the back seat to withdraw a rectangular pan.

"What kind?"

"Turtle cake."

Lindsey's tawny eyes went dreamy. "With caramel and nuts?"

"That's the one."

"Now I know you're staying even if I have to tie you up."

Molly managed a smile, some of her nerves settling.

Falling in step beside Lindsey, she walked up the grassy knoll to the pavilion.

Aunt Patsy bustled around near the food table, poking spoons into casseroles and salads. When she saw Molly, her face lit up.

"There's my girl." She rushed forward, wrapped Molly in a motherly hug and whispered, "Thank you, darling."

And Molly remembered all over again why she'd come. And why she would stay.

Along with Lindsey and Aunt Patsy she plunged into work, readying the potluck spread for the Seventh Cavalry, as Aunt Patsy called the gathered crowd.

She was slicing a pecan pie and listening

to Clare Thompson chatter about the upcoming bazaar when Aunt Patsy leaned toward her. "Chloe's here."

As she followed her aunt's gaze, a cold knot formed in her stomach.

Her sister stepped out of a church van and began unloading toddlers.

"You said she wasn't coming."

"That's what James told me yesterday."

Molly laid the pie knife aside. "Maybe I should leave."

"You will not." Aunt Patsy grabbed her upper arm. "Chloe knew you would be here, and she chose to come anyway. She saw you last weekend at church and this is no different."

Maybe Aunt Patsy was right. She and Chloe had managed to be in the same church building together without causing an explosion. Granted, they'd ignored each other and stayed on opposite sides of the building. Maybe they could do the same today.

Squaring her shoulders, she picked up the knife again and resumed cutting.

"Good girl."

Molly watched from beneath her lashes as her sister came up the rise. Long involved in the church's bus outreach to kids, Chloe was followed by members of her Sunday School class whose parents didn't attend.

Molly marveled that Chloe, who grieved so violently for her son, preferred to teach the little ones. Where Molly panicked around kids, her sister seemed to draw comfort.

Chloe, accompanied by her husband, clucked around the children like a mother hen. When her eyes found Molly, she stared long and hard, then hitched her chin in the air and herded the kids toward the sand pile.

Foolishly disappointed, Molly watched the thin woman move away from her. When would she stop hoping and longing that Chloe would forgive her? That they could once again share the special bond of sisterhood?

She turned aside, only to find Ethan watching her over a can of pop. Great. From one heartache to the other in zero point two seconds. Luckily, Deb Castor came up just then looking for volleyball recruits.

"Come on, Molly. We need another warm body on our team." Earrings swinging, Deb tugged Molly toward the net set up in back of the pavilion. "Tom's team is blitzing us, as usual."

Though husband and wife, Deb and Tom got a kick out of competing against each other.

Glad for the tension reliever, Molly trotted to the back court. Good-natured insults volleyed across the net long before the first serve. She relaxed and tossed a few back, feeling good to be in the midst of old acquaintances.

Hands on her knees, she waited while the other players got into position.

Suddenly, her arms tingled with awareness. She instinctively knew who stood next to her.

"Hi," Ethan said quietly when she glanced over at him.

"Hi." His eyes were incredibly blue today, as blue as the spring sky.

Heart in her throat, she had so much to say. She wanted to know how he was. What he'd been doing. How Laney was. She wanted to apologize for the sadness she detected in those gorgeous blue eyes of his, and to tell him what a difference he'd made in her life.

But, of course, she couldn't.

Tom's team served and the ball came at her, falling with a thud onto the sand.

"Sorry," she called, trotting to collect the ball and send it back to the other side.

If she was going to play this game, she didn't dare look at Ethan again.

She concentrated, and the next time the ball came her way, she leaped into action with a decent forearm pass. Ethan darted beneath her, slammed the ball up and over the net for a side out.

Without thinking about it they turned and slapped congratulatory high fives. As soon as they touched, Molly regretted the action. Touching him, looking at him, was killer.

Deb moved up to serve and everyone rotated. Ethan stepped to the net, leaving Molly in the back.

He looked great from her view. So good she missed the next ball that came in her direction. And the next.

"Time to eat." Pastor Cliff's voice boomed the news. Molly almost fainted with relief. Another five minutes of drooling over Ethan and she would be tempted to do something stupid.

Back beneath the pavilion, she slid in line behind Lindsey and took a paper plate. Pastor Cliff gave a short prayer and then the crowd surged forward like sharks after blood. Shoulders jostled, voices buzzed. A teenager put ice down Molly's back, and she yelped and danced, all to the delight of her tormentors.

She loved being here. She hated being here. Crazy, mixed-up woman that she was.

"I'll get you for that," she said, glaring in mock anger at the clutch of teenage boys who tried hard to appear innocent.

"You have admirers," a rich, purring voice said in her ear.

Her pulse leaped, warning her long before she looked that the speaker was Ethan. Even his aftershave, woodsy and dark, told on him.

"Teenagers like to pester. It has nothing to do with admiration."

His plate piled high with enough food to last Molly a week, he gestured toward an empty table under a shade tree.

"Sit with me. Tell me what you've been up to."

I'd love to.

"I don't think that's a good idea."

"It's only a hamburger."

She couldn't stop the smile. "That sounds a lot like, 'It's not a date.'"

His blue eyes danced at the memory. He

took her paper plate from her hand. "Get us a soda. Then come and sit. If at any point this feels like a date you can get up and run."

She hesitated. Had she come hoping this would happen? Was she that big a fool?

"Where's Laney?"

"With Karen." Both hands full, he hitched his chin toward the pastor's wife. "Want to get her?"

Molly let the suggestion slide. Yes, she desperately wanted to hold Laney, to smell her baby smell and kiss her soft skin. But that was a risk she couldn't take.

Just as spending more time with Ethan was a risk she couldn't take.

She reached for her plate, took it from him. "We'd better not, Ethan. I'm sorry."

Before she could change her mind she walked away, feeling his eyes on her back. Searching the tables for someone comfortable to sit with, she saw Lindsey and her family.

"Mind if I join you?" she asked.

Lindsey scooted to one side. "We'd love to have you."

Truth be told, her appetite had gone with Ethan, but she threw a leg over the concrete bench and sat. Lindsey's step-daughter,

Jade, beamed her good will. "My mommy's having a baby."

Jesse laughed. "Eat your burger, Butterbean, before I do." He pretended to reach for the sandwich. Jade squealed and jerked it away in a full body swing.

"You two kids stop fussing," Lindsey said, laughing with them.

Jesse slid an arm around her waist and hugged her close. "Yes, ma'am. We'll be good."

He winked at Jade, and Molly envied the love flowing through the little family.

She picked at her food, found it flavorless. Around the crowded table, the conversation flowed, but she felt no compunction to participate other than to smile or nod. Try as she might, she couldn't stop thinking about Ethan.

From where she sat, she could see the side of his face. Some girl she didn't know sat across from him. A bit of jealousy curled in her stomach, so she doused it with root beer and potato chips.

He leaned back and laughed. Molly watched, mesmerized. On his lap, Laney waved her chubby arms, grabbing at everything within her reach. Ethan efficiently thwarted her attempts to steal his potato chips, handed her a toy instead and kissed the top of her head.

Molly remembered the strength of those hands and the warmth of his mouth on hers.

"Why don't you go over there and sit with them?"

She jerked to awareness, embarrassed that Lindsey had caught her staring at Ethan like a sick dog.

"Not a good idea."

"Why not?" Lindsey asked. "I thought you two were a couple."

"Were. That's over."

"And that's too bad. He's a terrific guy."

Molly didn't need anyone to tell her how terrific he was. Pieces of her heart broke loose every time she thought of what might have been.

She bit into a forkful of potato salad, barely tasting the tangy mustard. The food was good but she'd lost her appetite, even for turtle cake.

Ethan liked her turtle cake. She wondered if he'd gotten a slice.

There he was again, in her head. She furtively slanted her eyes in his direction, trying not to draw attention.

As if he heard her thoughts, Ethan turned and captured her gaze with his.

She had to stop this nonsense. Now.

She stood abruptly, garnering curious glances from her table mates. "I think I'll take a walk."

Dumping her half-empty plate in the trash, she started toward the lake a hundred yards downhill from the pavilion. Trash littered the beachfront, an acceptable excuse for getting away from the crowd and Ethan's tempting presence. She found an empty sack and started picking up cans and bottles and paper along the water's edge.

The cloudy green water lapped against the shore in gentle waves. She inhaled, taking in the freshness of the air and the slightly fishy scent of the lake.

She hadn't been out here in a long time. Once she and her dad had fished for bass in this lake, and as kids she and Chloe had learned to swim here.

Gazing out across the wide expanse of Winding Stair Lake, she remembered. Good memories that no amount of heart-ache could erase.

A wave swelled and white-capped, pretty as a painting.

Something orange, a buoy perhaps, caught her attention.

She frowned and strained her eyes. No. Not a buoy. Something that ballooned up over the wave top and flapped with the motion.

A chill of fear skittered down her spine.

A shirt. An orange shirt. A very small orange shirt.

Surely, it wasn't attached to a person.

She squinted against the glare, her hand going to her mouth. "Oh, Lord. No."

A child's head bobbed up and down. The orange object was the bulge of his air-filled T-shirt holding him, barely, above the water.

Molly whirled toward the pavilion where Ethan walked toward a Dumpster, plate in hand.

"Ethan," she screamed. "There's a child in the water!"

Ethan whirled toward her voice. He dropped the plate and took off in a gallop. But he was more than a hundred yards away. The child didn't have that much time.

She looked back toward the lake. Only the orange shirt bobbed on the surface. The child's head had disappeared beneath the waves.

Like a bad dream, time froze. A child was going to die and Molly was the only one close enough to do anything.

Her heart accelerated into panic mode. Her throat constricted.

Another child was going to die. And it would be her fault—again.

Chapter Fifteen

"No!" she screamed and broke toward the lake, shedding her shoes and over-shirt as she ran.

She hit the water in a dead run. The icy cold sucked her breath away. Her pulse rattled wildly, threatening.

She would not, could not let the fear take over. A child's life was at stake.

With a silent prayer for help, she plunged beneath the murky water. Her body rebelled against the cold. Her calves tightened at the unexpected temperature drop.

Molly ignored everything but the need to get to the child.

She fought through the incoming current, training her eyes on that distant spot. Then the orange shirt disappeared. Molly dove beneath the surface, eyes wide and stinging as she frantically searched.

All the while, she prayed. "Show me where he is. Help me get to him in time. Help me. Help me."

An eternity seemed to pass while she thrashed beneath the waves. Her cold limbs grew heavy from exertion. Her chest felt as though it would explode.

Suddenly she glimpsed orange and, with one final burst of energy, lurched toward it.

Grabbing the loose shirt, she yanked the child's head above the water.

Molly's heart, already thundering from effort, nearly shattered.

He was nothing but a baby. A toddler, perhaps three years old. His eyes were closed. And his lips were blue.

"You're okay, baby," she said. But looking into his small, waxy white face she feared he was already dead.

Wrapping an arm around him, she lifted his limp body above the surface and, with every ounce of energy she could muster, raced toward shore. All the while, she remembered the last lifeless body she'd held.

Don't let another one die on me, Lord, she

prayed silently. *Not another one. He can't die. He won't die.*

The words became an internal chant as she stroked hard and fast toward the crowd gathered along the bank. Long before her feet touched bottom, Ethan, grim-faced and determined, came wading toward her. He shoved the water aside with power and impatience—as if he controlled the very waves.

Exhausted, she drew on the last of her strength to thrust the child across the short distance that separated her from Ethan.

Ethan yanked the toddler into his arms and ran back toward land, whipping the water aside with his powerful strides.

Molly followed, relieved that Ethan was there to help. He'd know what to do. Numb and cold and terrified, she watched as his broad back bent over the boy and puffed a breath into the tiny nose and mouth.

Let him live. Let him live. She wasn't sure if she thought the words or spoke them.

When she stumbled ashore someone draped a tablecloth over her shoulders. She realized then that her body shook wildly. Water dripped from her hair into her eyes and mouth.

But she didn't care. All that mattered was the boy.

She pushed through the ring of onlookers to where Ethan was performing CPR. She prayed. And begged.

Other than whispered prayers, a hush hung over the circle. The time seemed an eternity.

From somewhere nearby came a woman's keening cry. Molly wished she would stop. Wailing meant they had given up. And they couldn't give up. Not yet. Not ever.

Another eternity passed while Ethan pressed the narrow chest and breathed into a nose and mouth so small that the rescuer's lips easily eclipsed them.

Shoulders tight as stretched leather, teeth chattering, Molly commanded, "Breathe, baby, breathe."

As if her words were what he waited for, the toddler coughed. Ethan quickly turned him on his side and a gush of water spewed forth.

Then the most beautiful sound in the world filled the clearing. The little one began to cry. In seconds, he was calling for his mama.

Molly went limp, weeping with relief into her chilled palms.

"We got to him in time. He should be

okay," she heard Ethan say. "But you need to take him to the ER. Have him checked over to be sure."

It was then that Molly saw her sister standing white-faced and horrified. Tears streaming from her eyes, she stood riveted to the scene.

"I only turned my back to get Tracy a drink," Chloe said. "How did Corey get into the water so fast? How did..."

The keening noise issued from her lips, and Molly realized it was Chloe she'd heard before.

Her stricken gaze fell on Molly. "I nearly caused a child's death. If you hadn't seen him— If you hadn't gone after him..."

Hysterical sobs broke loose and racked her thin body.

Regardless of what had gone on before, Molly couldn't ignore her sister's cries. No one understood the feeling of despair and remorse and horror any better than she did.

Gently, she touched her sister's quaking shoulder.

"No, sis, don't. Don't blame yourself. Sometimes bad things just happen."

Miraculously, as she comforted her sister, Molly, too, was comforted. The truth of her words soaked into the deepest part of her mind and blossomed there. *Sometimes bad things just happen.*

A shudder rippled through Chloe. She lifted her teary face. "How can you be nice to me after the way I've treated you?"

"Easy." Letting the tablecloth fall, Molly held out her arms. "I love you, sis."

Chloe stumbled forward and fell against the much-shorter Molly. Her words, punctuated with sobs, were the redemption Molly had long prayed for.

"I'm sorry. So sorry for blaming you." Molly realized she spoke of Zack. "It wasn't your fault. I always knew that. Will you forgive me?"

Though she was tired to the core, Molly couldn't remember when she'd felt such joy or release. She rubbed Chloe's bony shoulder in comforting circles.

"There is nothing to forgive. All I want is to have my sister back again."

Chloe pulled away and managed a damp and tremulous smile. "I've missed you so much."

Most of the other people had wandered off, following the accident victim, murmuring in low, shocked tones. Chloe's husband appeared at her side.

His own complexion, usually ruddy, was pale. "You girls all right?"

Her eyes were red, her face streaked with tears, but Chloe's smile bloomed for real. "More than all right. Everything is going to work out now, James. I promise."

"Thank God." He closed his eyes briefly. When he opened them, Molly recognized her own hurt, confusion, and finally relief in him. James had suffered, too. Everyone suffered from unresolved bitterness.

"Yes," Ethan said, moving up to stand beside Molly. "Thank God."

James's smile was gentle and loving as he slipped an arm around his wife. "Come on, honey. We could all use some rest. But first we need to round up these little tots and get them home."

"I want to go to the hospital to make sure Corey's all right." Chloe's tear-filled eyes followed a car streaking away with Corey inside.

"Then let's get going."

With a final hug and a promise to call tomorrow, Chloe and James started up the rise toward the dispersing crowd.

Molly's emotions were a jumble as she watched her sister walk away. Fear, relief, joy and, most of all, hope swirled around inside her. As awful as it had been, the near-tragedy had given her hope that she and Chloe could be sisters again.

Shivering with reaction and cold, Molly bent to retrieve the tablecloth. As her shaking fingers touched the vinyl, Ethan swooped it up. He placed the soft flannel backing around her shoulders, along with his strong arm.

"You were amazing." He gazed down at her with an expression that almost made her forget how scared she'd been.

"So were you."

"No. I mean you were more than amazing. You saved that little boy from a certain drowning. You didn't panic, Molly. You took control and did what had to be done to save his life."

The truth washed over her. She'd been scared, but she hadn't panicked. She had faced a crisis with a child, and she had not crumbled into hysteria. She had not lost control.

Both she and the little boy were fine.

For the first time in two years, her

thoughts became crystal-clear as the truth awakened within her. She turned her face into the warmth and protection that was Ethan's chest. "I have been such an idiot."

He said nothing, only rubbed his hands up and down her shivering arms. And then, as if he understood, he heaved a great sigh and enfolded her.

Burrowing close, Molly absorbed his wonderful warmth, the scent of his skin, the essence of him. "I've been scared for so long that I had forgotten how to live. Only an idiot would hold on to crippling fear and let go of you and Laney."

His grip tightened.

"Are you saying what I hope you're saying?" he asked, his voice a deep purr of hope against her ear.

"I need you in my life, Ethan. You and Laney. Will you forgive me?"

"Forgive you? All I ever wanted was to make you see yourself as I see you. A woman of compassion and love. Brave and strong." He rocked her back and forth. "The past is the past. Let it stay there."

The past is the past. Yes, she could accept that now.

Tilting her head back, she contemplated

his wonderful face. She was incredibly blessed to be loved by him. Why hadn't she seen that before?

She raised a fingertip to tenderly trace the long scar over his eyebrow. "I love you, Ethan Hunter."

"Scars and all?" he asked.

"Scars and all."

The doubt lingering in his expression faded away. He rocked her back and forth and said, "I think you've seen the end of the panic attacks, don't you?"

"Maybe. But even if I haven't, I won't let them interfere with us again. I'll get through them and keep going. Someday they'll only be a bad memory."

A sigh of relief shuddered through him. She'd hurt him, and yet he was here, ready to give her another chance.

"We'll get through them together," he murmured, placing a kiss on her wet hair. "Marry us, Molly. Me and Laney."

Her heart slammed into her ribcage. Her breath came in short puffs, but this time only happiness came along for the ride.

It wasn't the kind of proposal she'd dreamed of, but somehow it was perfect. "Okay."

Ethan tilted her away from him a little and stared into her eyes. "Did you just agree to be my wife? And Laney's mom?"

"Yes, I did."

With a whoop of joy, Ethan lifted her high into the air, twirling her round and round. In the distance, their friends turned startled faces in their direction.

Molly didn't mind. Cold and wet and absolutely ecstatic, she laughed down at this man who'd helped her escape from her frozen prison and step into the warm sunlight that was life and love.

Slowly Ethan lowered her to the sand, pulled her close, and warmed her shivering lips with his.

From the rise a hundred yards away, Molly heard the sound of applause.

Epilogue

A winter storm watch had been issued by the National Weather Service for the entire quadrant of southeastern Oklahoma. As yet, nothing fell in Winding Stair and the temperatures hovered above the freezing mark. None of this mattered one whit to Ethan. Like the postman, no amount of rain, sleet or snow could keep him from his appointed rounds. Not today. No way.

Heart thump-thumping like the blades of a chopper, he stood in front of the Winding Stair Chapel's sanctuary wearing his Sunday best and waiting for a glimpse of his bride.

With his brother beside him as best man and his parents beaming approval from the second pew on the left, he experienced an overwhelming sense of gratitude for all that had transpired over the course of a year.

On the advice of family and pastor he and Molly had waited most of a year to take their vows. Time to know one another better, months of counseling and spiritual growth, months to confirm what they already knew: God had blessed them each with exactly the right helpmate.

He heard titters, saw the smiles of indulgent amusement, and followed the guests' turned heads to see his baby girl, now over a year old, barreling toward him. Mouth wide open, her blue eyes danced with the thrill of spotting her daddy.

Ethan grinned. Since she'd learned to walk, Laney had one gear and it was stuck on run. An awkward, fall-down-at-any-moment run.

Dressed like an angel in some kind of white fluffy material Molly had chosen, she wore tiny gossamer wings and a head wreath of flowers and streaming purple ribbons.

She arrived in front of him with her arms stretched upward. He swooped her into his arms, planted a kiss on her nose, and hoped she continued to behave. But whether she did or not made no difference, really. Molly had insisted Laney be part of the ceremony. After all, when he'd proposed he asked her to marry both of them. And so she would.

His chest filled with happiness. Until Molly came along, other than raising his child, he'd had no plans, no dreams for his future. He'd been stuck in a rut as surely as he'd been stuck in the ice on the night they met.

Now, they had plans and dreams together. They would build a house, a big one with plenty of rooms. Someday they'd have more kids.

With his blessing, Molly and her sister had opened their dream craft store. And Molly had stolen his heart even more by insisting on caring for Laney while she worked. As a result, the bond was so strong between woman and child that he'd suffered a twinge of jealousy the first time Laney cried for Molly instead of him.

And because of Molly's encouragement, he would be a full-time pilot again come spring. Truly he was a blessed man.

The music changed just then, and with a lurch, he recognized the chords announcing the bride's entrance. She took his breath, did his Molly. Simple and elegant, she looked like a snow queen floating toward him.

Laney strained toward the beautiful apparition, babbling wildly. Ethan considered doing the same.

Molly had watched as her daughter-to-be raced toward Ethan and leaped into his arms. Her own excitement level on overdrive, she wanted to follow suit.

Instead, she took her time, gliding down the aisle, giving tiny waves and big smiles to all the friends and family gathered in the chapel. She stopped at the third pew to hug Aunt Patsy and at the second to kiss her mom.

Chloe, her matron of honor, waited beside the pastor, playing one-handed patty-cake with Laney.

So many things had changed for the better. Her faith was stronger. She had her family back. Fear no longer ruled her life.

All because of Ethan.

She glided into place and turned toward him, unable to keep her eyes off the man who would finally become her husband today. Movie-star handsome in his rented tux, he winked at her, his smile wide and white and jubilant as he handed Laney into Chloe's waiting arms.

The soloist began to sing, "Make My Heart Your Home," their promise to each other.

Molly leaned her head toward Ethan and whispered, "We may spend our honeymoon iced in."

"Sounds good to me," he murmured against her ear. "I know this perfect little farm outside of town. We could pop some popcorn. Play a little Scrabble. Snuggle in front of the fireplace."

Suppressing a giggle, she whispered back, "Sounds good to me, too."

And it did. It truly did. How fitting to return as husband and wife to the place where God had shaken their worlds and led them to each other. The place where both of them had begun to thaw.

The music ended and Pastor Cliff began to speak. Molly heard nothing except the singing in her heart.

Yes, the painful past seemed light years ago.

Ethan turned in her direction and smiled.

Lost in the blue eyes of her beloved, Molly placed her hand in his outstretched one and let the future begin.

* * * * *

Dear Reader,

The idea for this book first came to me out of the blue several years ago. At the time I had never met anyone who had lost a child to SIDS. Then a terrible thing happened. I had written the first chapter and was fiddling with the rest of the plot when my niece's seemingly healthy baby boy died in his sleep, a tiny victim to Sudden Infant Death Syndrome. The pain for the entire family was so excruciating that I felt it inappropriate to finish the story at that time. I put it away only to come back to it recently. Although *A Very Special Delivery* is entirely fictional, I hope I've adequately and respectfully conveyed the terrible feeling of shock and loss and grief that families suffer during such a time. Most importantly, I hope it conveys the comfort and healing that only God can give after such a tragedy.

Please let me know if you enjoy Molly's and Ethan's story. You can reach me c/o Steeple Hill, 233 Broadway, Suite 1001, New York, NY 10279, or through my Web site, www.lindagoodnight.com.

With blessings,

Linda Goodnight

QUESTIONS FOR DISCUSSION

1. There are different levels of forgiveness represented in this story. Can you identify them? Molly, Ethan and Chloe all struggled with forgiveness in one way or another. Which character do you think needed forgiveness the most? Why?
2. Have you ever dealt with unforgiveness? Were you the one who needed forgiveness, or the one who needed to forgive? What did you do to come to grips with the problem? Is forgiveness an act of will or an act of grace?
3. Both Molly and Ethan are consumed with guilt. Discuss what each felt guilty about. How did their guilt cripple relationships with others? How did it affect their relationship with each other?
4. Do you think a person should be held accountable for the mistakes he/she makes before accepting Christ?
5. Discuss the meaning of the scripture, "Whatsoever things you sow, that will you also reap." How does it apply to Ethan? To Chloe? Can this verse have a positive as well as a negative meaning? How have you experienced this verse in your own life?
6. Molly perceives that her church friends blame her for her nephew's death. Is this true? Why do you think she feels this way?
7. The Bible says, "Perfect love casts out fear." What does that mean? How does this apply to Molly?

8. Ethan encounters a woman at the Easter pageant who makes him have second thoughts about his relationship with Molly. Why do you suppose she said the things she did? Have you ever dealt with a self-righteous person?
9. Which of the characters in *A Very Special Delivery* did you identify with most? Why?
10. If a stranger appeared on your doorstep during a terrible storm such as occurred in the book, would you be willing to give them shelter? Why or why not? What does scripture say about this? Do you think that applies in today's world?